# TREASURE OF THE LONE STAR

Like everybody in Puchero County, Sheriff Adam Kane supposed that the stolen Aztec jewellery lay at the bottom of a swamp. But Kane began to doubt this when a number of faces showed up, including the notorious master-thief, Colonel Alonzo Barris. The dangerous combination of the thieves alongside a murder and an attempt on Kane's life really got the sheriff worried. Could he uncover the mystery before the killer struck again and all hell was let loose?

TREASURE OF THE
LONE STAR

Like everybody in Ranchero County,
Sheriff Adam Kane supposed that
the stolen Aztec jewellery lay at the
bottom of a swamp. But Kane began
to doubt this when a number of faces
showed up, including the notorious
master-thief, Colonel Alonzo Barris.
The dangerous combination of the
thieves alongside a murder and an
attempt on Kane's life really got the
sheriff worried. Could he uncover
the mystery before the killer struck
again and all hell was let loose?

BILL WADE

# TREASURE OF THE LONE STAR

*Complete and Unabridged*

# LINFORD
*Leicester*

First published in Great Britain in 1997 by
Robert Hale Limited
London

First Linford Edition
published 1998

The right of Bill Wade to be identified
as the author of this work has been asserted
by him in accordance with the
Copyright, Designs and Patents Act, 1988

British Library CIP Data

Wade, Bill *1928–*
Treasure of the Lone Star.—Large print ed.—
Linford western library
1. Western stories
2. Large type books
I. Title
823.9′14 [F]

ISBN 0–7089–5331–X

Published by
F. A. Thorpe (Publishing) Ltd.
Anstey, Leicestershire

Set by Words & Graphics Ltd.
Anstey, Leicestershire
Printed and bound in Great Britain by
T. J. International Ltd., Padstow, Cornwall

This book is printed on acid-free paper

# 1

Adam Kane, the Sheriff of Rockford, Texas, was feeling irritated as he stood, with feet set apart and hands linked behind his back, at the window of his office which looked out on the main street of the town. Three times this morning he had seen a face pass by which he had not seen in the last seven years and would have been happy never to see again. Tony Essen had never been any good. In his early adult years, before the Civil War, he had been a petty thief and suspected of rustling; but, in the years since the conflict had ended, it had been reported that he had graduated to much bigger and far more serious crimes than before, and that he now rode as a senior member of Captain Jack Starbuck's gang.

Frowning, Kane shifted his position a little and ground his teeth. Doubtless the law up country had proof of Essen's wrongdoing, but there was none here in Rockford. Indeed, the man wasn't wanted for any crime in Puchero County — of which Rockford wasn't even the county town, so Kane didn't have the county sheriff's authority to step outside, stop the man on the sidewalk, and tell him to get out of these parts and stay out. Essen had done nothing here in recent times to warrant censure, though his boozy cheeks did suggest that he had spent a lot of money on whiskey this morning; but free-spending of that kind could only make him popular in town — especially with the several saloonkeepers who managed to make a fat living in the salty airs which blew in from the Gulf of Mexico.

There was the man again. It was almost as if he were advertising his presence. Just what in tarnation was he doing in Rockford? The town had never liked him, and he was on the record as having told the editor of the *Puchero Echo* that Rockford was 'full of psalm-singing hypocrites, virtue and bad smells, and that he hated the place worse'n hell'. What, then, could a sour-mouthed malcontent of his gabby gifts be seeking in this centre of his loathing? But he would not be here by choice — he would have been sent. Yet that, too, begged a reason. Assuming that Essen was idling around at Jack Starbuck's command, he could hardly be sizing up the Starbuck gang's next job. There was nothing in Rockford to inspire the appetite of big-time criminals. The town bank obviously didn't hold enough to be worth the risk of taking, there was no business that kept a hundred dollars on the premises — no railroad, no stage depot — and the nearest mines were many a mile away. Okay; there was the fact of it. Rockford was small beer, and not worth any attention from the criminal fraternity. Yet Tony Essen was here — and an eye ought to be kept on him.

Kane hitched uneasily at his gunbelt. His irritation was getting worse by the moment. He couldn't keep making half-assed excuses for any of it. There was crime in this somewhere. He could actually feel it as a weight upon his shoulders. Maybe a bushwhacking was intended. Perhaps somebody in town had offended Captain Jack. It was possible. Quarrels and feuds were springing up all the time. Even in a small place like this, the law could not keep track of all that was going on. But Essen as a bushwhacker? Hell, no! Kane and he had served together in the same Texas infantry regiment during the war, and Essen had had the reputation of being a clumsy soldier and an indifferent shot. Such defects hardly made a sharp-shooter, and any man who tried to become one, when lacking the necessary stealth and guncraft, was liable to end up as the only victim of his evil ambition. Yet the world was full of fools with puffed up opinions of what they could do, and Tony Essen might have become one. Yes, he must be watched — perhaps to save him from himself. It could be done discreetly. After all, it was a sheriff's first duty to keep crime off the street; and he could only be blamed if he didn't.

Kane heard a movement that came from behind the rear wall of his office. He had forgotten that Jim Derby, his deputy, was still working back there in the cell block. Jim, a deliberate character at the best of times, wasn't pushing himself today. He had been turning over the mattresses on the cell bunks for the last twenty minutes, and it would probably take him as long again to gather up the blankets for their semi-annual trip to the laundry. Not that Jim's tardiness mattered a damn. There wasn't a whole heap to do most days — some paperwork, a few patrols, and the simple chores that fell the lot of every man and woman. Serving the law in Rockford was chiefly a matter of putting in the time, but twelve-hour shifts, however you planned or overlapped them, made the whole business pretty much of a bore most weeks. Just once in a while something happened — and today could be the day. 'Hey — Jim!'

Derby's plump, merry-eyed face appeared at the entrance to the jailhouse a moment or two later. 'You hollered, Adam?' he inquired.

'I did,' Kane responded. 'Watch the shop.'

'You going out, suh?'

Kane turned his eyes to heaven. 'How did you figure that out?'

'Brains, I guess,' Derby returned in the same spirit of cheerful disparagement. 'You've seen him, eh?'

'Several times. Didn't know you had.'

'Spotted him on my way here. He was coming out of the Packet Rat saloon.'

'You didn't say.'

'Didn't want to talk up trouble,' Derby replied. 'I knew you'd spot him before long.'

'That's what I call real helpful, Jim.'

'We've nothing on him, Adam.'

'I've a notion we will have before this day's out.'

'It's never been your policy to hound a visitor.'

'He's up to no good in Rockford,' Kane said, moving to his left and opening the street door, 'And we both know it.'

'I'll be watching the shop.'

'Mind you do, pardner,' the sheriff responded, a cautionary note in his voice. 'Don't you let me come back here and find you've nodded off in my chair.'

Shutting the door behind him, Kane chuckled wryly down the front of his shirt. It wasn't much good trying to throw a scare into Jim Derby. Short of direct orders — which he always obeyed adequately enough — he would do the deputy sheriff's job according to his lights and nobody else's. The amazing part was that he almost never made a mistake. Even in failing to report that

7

he had seen Tony Essen in town, he had wisely left the sheriff to do his own spotting and then make up his own mind as to how the matter should be handled. It remained true that they had nothing on Essen, and that a citizen had the right to complain of harassment by the law. The responsibility for whatever happened next was Adam Kane's, and his alone. Maybe Jim Derby *was* plain smart.

Kane gazed along the street. Tony Essen was still visible on the sidewalk. He had just stepped out of a shop doorway and accosted a good-looking blonde girl. The female was dressed in a straw hat, a dress of yellow gingham, and boots of alligator skin. She was in her middle twenties and at her absolute best, with her peachy complexion, straight nose, wide, shapely mouth and vivid blue eyes. She was another person that Kane knew well enough — though here again he hadn't seen her in some considerable time — and he recalled that back in their schooldays, though a few years older than Jill Pedlar, Tony Essen had been openly fond of the girl. From his expression now, his feelings had not changed; but, sadly for him, now as then, Jill Pedlar had no similar liking for him and was fending off his attempts to hold her by the shoulders and look deep into her face while talking to her. The sight of the girl wriggling her upper body and brushing at the man's arms with her hands incensed Kane, and he saw in it, as if heavensent, the opportunity to send Essen packing without providing Tony or anybody else with a reason to question the fairness of the dismissal.

His tread picking up speed, Kane reached the spot where Jill Pedlar and Tony Essen stood together — still intermittently going through their 'grab and denial' routine — within half a minute, and the sheriff said: 'Get your hands off her, Tony, and leave town fast. If I find you're still in Rockford ten minutes from now, I'll lock you up

9

in a cell and keep you there for a day or two.'

'What the blazes is this?' Tony Essen demanded, taking a step backwards and looking both angry and bewildered. 'You can't do that! Who — ? Oh, it's you, Adam Kane! I heard a couple of years ago they'd made you sheriff of this muck-heap! You sure haven't changed much! You always were a great bullyin' bastard who couldn't keep his nose out of other folks' affairs!' He spat deliberately into the dirt between his feet. 'Lock me up, you say? On what charge, eh? You tell me what charge. If it's just you being who you are and I being who — '

'Assault!' Kane cut in savagely. 'I'll lock you up for indecent assault! You can't go around pawing girls!'

'Indecent assault!' Essen snarled, his black eyes popping and his bared teeth dripping as, undoubtedly fuelled by alcohol, his mounting rage began to rob him of his reason. 'I haven't harmed a hair of Jill's head — '

'Well, Jill?' Kane again interrupted.

'He hasn't harmed a hair of my head,' the girl admitted thinly. 'But — but he twice tried to have his way with me out at my house yesterday afternoon.'

'Rape you?' Kane prompted. 'Are you saying rape you? We hang men for that. Further up the coast, along Port Arthur way, they hanged a guy for that last year.'

'You lying bitch!' Essen raved, his total fury an awful thing to see as he turned it all on the girl and sent her cringeing away from him. 'I tried to kiss you — I only tried to kiss you. I was trying to comfort you! You were sobbing like a baby, you ninny! I rode up and found you like that.'

'My dad has just died,' Jill Pedlar said brokenly. 'You were a help, Tony, but then you tried to take advantage.' She shook her head, a great gulp emphasizing the renewed grief in the tears that now ran copiously down her cheeks. 'Just go away, Tony. Do what

11

the sheriff says — leave town!'

'Oh, no!' Kane announced implacably. 'He isn't going to get away with this that easily. No, sir! Will you prefer a charge of attempted rape against him, Jill?'

'No,' the girl faltered, 'th-that would b-be taking it much too far. I — I haven't been harmed.'

'He could get ten years all the same,' Kane grated. 'He's a public enemy, Jill. You'd be doing folk everywhere a service. If he got his just desserts he'd have been put away for life or hanged from the gallows long ago!'

'Do you hear that, Tony?' the girl quavered. 'You're a wicked man, far gone in crime, and that was the law telling you. G-go somewhere new — repent of your past — before it's t-too late. The law will get you in the end, sure as fate!'

'Aw, you crazy little wildcat!' Essen blurted, lifting his knuckles in a threat to backhand the blonde. 'Never will the day dawn that Adam Kane has the best of me! He's just a great big stupid ox! The law is full of empty-headed nincompoops like him! I've run rings round posses made up of Adam Kanes a hundred times!' The young man's lips worked and his eyes rolled, showing bloodshot edges. 'Can't you see what he's up to, Jilly? The ugly galoot is tryin' to use you! He wants you to provide him with the excuse to lock me up on a trumped up charge. I've done nothing wrong in Puchero county — and well he knows it!'

'Stop yelling, Tony!' Jill Pedlar advised. 'You're calling the attention of half the town to us. Besides, it seems to me you just confessed to having done a lot of evil things elsewhere. I've half a mind to tell the whole truth about how you mauled me — with my father not yet cold in the bed you threw me across.'

'Pah!' Essen screamed, his fury tipping him right over the edge this time, and he let fly with the backhander which he had essayed before; but the sheriff thrust him off balance at the same instant and, catching a spur against the edge of the boardwalk adjacent, he went down, shoulder-blades hitting the ground with some force and his parted legs flying up to reveal the saddleworn seat of his trousers — a spectacle which earned him a round of derisive haw-hawing from a watcher nearby.

The laughter appeared to inflame Essen's boozy madness anew. He sprang erect and, without allowing himself even a moment of recovery time, flung himself at the sheriff with fists flying. He wasn't the biggest of men — and fell short of Kane's six-feet two by at least four inches — but he was muscular and broad-chested, a man hardened by army service and recent years spent in the saddle. He was physically fit and nobody's pushover, but his inborn clumsiness and lack of fistic instruction made his attack an open and flat-footed one. Kane simply blocked the other's swinging arms with his own and, stepping through the assault, put a leg at the back of Essen's legs and collided with his adversary chest to chest, using his own two-hundred pounds of muscle and best beef like a battering-ram, and over went Essen again, landing much as he had the first time and obviously knocking whatever wind he had left out of himself.

He lay back in the dirt, swallowing and gasping, and all kinds of expressions crossed his squarish, small-featured face, with its devil's eyebrows and thin moustache, and he opened and shut his dark eyes repeatedly to renew their focus. Then he sat up and bowed his head between his thighs, swearing to himself in the foulest language.

'You can cut that out as fast as you like, Tony!' Kane reproved. 'There's a lady present, and I'm not keen on dirty swearing myself.'

'Yeah, yeah,' Essen muttered.

Kane offered a hand to help him up. 'You've done it now, you know. The

15

sentence for attacking a peace officer is usually six months. It's time you learned to curb that temper of yours.'

Essen took the sheriff's proffered hand, gripping as Kane did the same, and the spirit of violence seemed to have left him. It appeared to Kane that Essen's two recent falls — and lessons in his own lack of pugilistic proficiency — had left him shaken up and rather subdued; but therein was the sheriff's mistake; for Essen was no sooner upright again than he threw a left hook at the lawman's chin and this time landed his blow on target and with full force.

As his brain darkened momentarily and he felt his knees start giving out, Kane threw back his left palm to catch himself should he hit the ground, but Tony Essen's persisting grasp on the hand which the sheriff had extended to help him up in fact kept Kane erect. He bowed his jaw in anticipation of another punch similar to the last one, and it came quickly enough, but he caught this blow on the side of the face and it did no more than bruise him. He quickly received further punishment of the same kind — the punches carrying an increasing desperation with them now — but he absorbed them all and, as his head cleared, tore himself free from Essen's grasp and waded into his enemy, doubling him up with blows to the belly and then belting him about the face, splitting his lips and eyebrows and squashing his nose.

With his enemy reeling and groggy, Kane slowed the overwhelming nature of his attack and began to take his time about what he was doing, selecting the moves and blows that would hurt Essen most. He was angry at the fashion in which his earlier attempt to be merciful had been spurned and then deliberately taken advantage of by his opponent. For that more than anything else, Kane was determined to give Essen the kind of hiding that he would ever remember — and he had just made up his mind that this beating was going to end with a knock-out punch — when Essen proved himself capable of further treachery by snatching out the revolver holstered on his right hip.

The sheriff, who had been intent only on doing battle with his fists, realized that he had again been the victim of his own basic fair play, and the barrel of Essen's pistol was already swinging at him as he tried to sway backwards out of its reach.

The evasive movement, started just too late, failed to save him entirely — but did partially thwart his enemy's obvious intention of braining him — for the muzzle of Essen's revolver did no more than clip the peak of his skull and drop him straight to his knees.

Still in possession of his senses, Kane was nevertheless filled with a sensation of paralysis. Pins-and-needles numbed his limbs and smothered most of the normal nerve impulses there. Kane realized that he was in a mess, and figured that, once Essen perceived that he was no longer able to rise again, the smaller man would finish the job with another clubbing blow or a bullet through the brain.

Reacting instinctively, Kane tried to reach for his own gun, but saw almost at once that his effort was unnecessary, for Essen had already faced about and was off down the street in a splay-footed run that soon drew itself together and speeded up as he covered ground.

Then he was clear of the immediate scene and headed swiftly for the western end of the main street, an escaper that nobody dared intercept.

His own physical sensations now improving rapidly, Kane wobbled erect and stood briefly irresolute; then, hardening his mind in every respect — since right was clearly on his side — he drew and cocked his revolver, pretty sure that he could bring Essen down before the running man passed completely out of range; but, just as he was about to lift his revolver and take aim, Jill Pedlar stepped between

19

him and his target, whispering: 'Let him go.'

'Get out of the way!' Kane hissed, trying to put her aside.

'You were going to let him go,' the blonde persisted, resisting the sheriff perceptibly.

'Are you out of your — ?'

'Don't make me responsible for a man's life,' she begged.

Looking over Jill Pedlar's head, Kane accepted the sincerity of her plea, but he also saw that the decision of whether or not to shoot no longer need be made. Tony Essen, coming to the town's last hitching rail on the left, had just hopped astride a horse — presumably his own mount — and had put his head down and was now galloping flat out for the brownish contours of the salt-tainted pastures that crossed the near distance.

He could only let the man go — for the moment. But he wished that Jill Pedlar had not interfered. It made him wonder about her.

# 2

Kane eased the hammer of his revolver off cock and thrust the weapon back into its holster. Then he touched the spot above the centre of his forehead where the muzzle of Tony Essen's pistol had clipped him. A considerable bump was present, and he winced; but the skin had not been broken and it was evident that no real harm had been done. Now he took Jill Pedlar by the arm and said: 'You do realize that I could arrest you for what you just did?'

'Why, certainly,' the girl responded, mocking him a little with her widened eyes. 'But you wouldn't, would you?'

'I guess not,' Kane admitted, grunting out a couple of reflective chuckles. 'Be hard to make the charges stick — when all you tried to do was make sure that I wasn't hurt?'

'Exactly, Sheriff,' Jill Pedlar agreed archly. 'Tony is a bad man — as everybody is well aware — but he wasn't the only sinner present just now.'

'Are you telling me, Jill, that you think I was using his behaviour towards you as an excuse to arrest him?'

'Weren't you?'

Kane stood and thought hard about that. The question was one that he realized he couldn't answer with total honesty. So he said: 'It's all part of the game, girl. Tony Essen was a worry. I believe he was in Rockford this morning for a purpose. Sorry, but I don't reckon it was you.'

'Why not?' the girl asked. 'He'd proved he was smitten, and it wouldn't have been hard to work out that I'd probably be in town this morning to visit the undertaker about my father's funeral.'

'It fits well enough,' Kane admitted, 'and you may even believe it. You always were a vain baggage, Jill Pedlar.'

'Was I, Adam Kane?' the blonde sighed. 'I'm a woman grown, and that's a fact, but I haven't had much of a chance to exercise my wiles as yet.'

'I guess you haven't,' Kane allowed. 'I'll warrant life's kept you among the more virtuous. You've been stuck out there — on the edge of that damned three-fingered swamp — Pedlar's Claw, they call it, after your father's crippled hand — all your born days, just looking after your pa and growing things in that garden plot of yours. Even Jezebel would have found that a life like that cramped her style.' He passed an eye up and down her neat but soberly dressed figure. 'You're no scarlet woman. Had you been, you'd never have got rid of Tony Essen before he'd done you the mischief he intended. How did you get rid of him?'

'I screamed,' she answered, 'and I also put a knee into him where one of the girls at school once told me it hurt a boy plenty. I think he must have business around these parts other than me. I had the feeling I was an afterthought — a way of passing a few hours. He wasn't to know that dad was breathing his last as he rode up to our front door.'

'That begins to sound like the truth,' Kane remarked. 'Essen didn't say — or even hint at — what he'd come to Puchero County for?'

'No.'

'Could be important, Jill.'

'Honestly, no.'

'That leaves me about where I was before,' Kane growled, more to himself than his companion. 'There's nothing around here that's worth stealing, and nobody who needs killing — except me, of course. So why the hell was he kicking his heels on my patch? Maybe I'm missing something in all this. I'm starting to get the feeling that I am.'

'People come and go,' Jill Pedlar reminded. 'Sometimes they get a yearning to see old places and faces.'

'Tony?'

'He's human, isn't he?'

'I question that. If he is, it's only just.'

'Oh, I think it's a little more than just,' the blonde said, clearly going out of her way to be fair. 'Shame at how he'd tried to bed me yesterday afternoon did play its part in making him go away.'

'If you say so,' Kane said doubtfully. 'When I knew you years ago, Jill, you were never a liar.'

'Yes,' she sighed. 'We did know each other, didn't we, when I was a youngster picking flowers and you were a fine soldier boy home on furlough in grey?' She glanced westwards. 'I ought to be getting back home.'

'What's there?'

'I locked a dead man in.'

'You can't help him any more,' Kane assured her gravely. 'You've made your sacrifice. There's just the funeral left. What are you going to do with your future?'

'I don't know,' Jill Pedlar admitted.

'Dad hasn't left me with much. His occupation didn't bring the money rolling in. He caught alligators, cured their skins beside the bayou, and made bags and boots and such goods out of the hides. We got by. Perhaps I'll live hand-to-mouth. There are many fish to be hooked, rabbits to be snared, and antelope to be shot. I shan't starve, Sheriff. I can fend for myself.'

Kane felt a reaction within him to the woman's strength and self-confidence. It could have been the dawning of something new or the renewal of something old. He wasn't sure, but decided that it didn't matter which. Jill Pedlar was not only beautiful, but she had the makings of a fine and able person. Her life must not be wasted. It should not be allowed to fade into buckskins and a leathery skin and wispy hair to match. She had come back into his orbit this morning, and he felt a certain responsibility for her. Then, with that sense of moral obligation, arrived an inspiration of a kind. If she had undeveloped talents — for which there might be no market — her abilities as a housekeeper were tried and tested, so they should be worth a living. Kane knew of an old man in the town — a Mr Henry Thompson, a bank manager from Galveston who had retired to Rockford — who needed one, and had said that he was prepared to pay better than the going rate for one that suited him and was not afraid of work. 'I've got an idea,' Kane announced, frankly a little pleased with himself.

'You have?' Jill Pedlar said, sounding both mystified and a trifle amused. 'To do with me?'

'To do with you, yes,' he responded briskly. 'But we can't go on standing out here in the middle of the main street and jabbering away like we've been doing.'

'I suppose not.'

'Will you come along to the restaurant with me?' Kane invited. 'We can share a pot of coffee and a plate of toast. Did you eat any breakfast before you came out?'

'No, I wasn't hungry.'

'Are you now?'

She thought about it. 'Yes.'

'That settles it then,' the sheriff said; and, taking her by the left elbow, he began steering her down the street in the direction of the 'Blue Bay' restaurant.

The blonde moved willingly enough, and they soon reached a brick building which stood on the left of the way and had a greater air of permanency than most of those in the vicinity. It also carried its name and a suitable motif above the door, while the paintwork was generally good and ivy and wisteria clung to the front wall. The sheriff and the girl walked in, and a bell on a spring above the entrance rang out shrilly to announce their arrival. They went to a table which stood behind a window that looked out on the street and there sat down, facing each other across the condiments and a glass vase of faded flowers. A middle-aged waitress stepped up at once, all smiles and sweetness, and took the sheriff's order. Then she hurried off in the direction of the kitchen, showing a like willingness to fetch what he required.

Kane cleared his throat. Without any preamble, he told Jill Pedlar his idea and added: 'If you want to work for Henry Thompson, it would bring you into town. Put you among people. Give you the chance to meet folk of your own age. There isn't much here, as they say, but we have dances and sports from time to time, and the ladies have their quilting parties and spelling B's. There's a chapel too, if you're of the mind.' He paused, smiling at the eyes but wry of mouth, then concluded in jest: 'Why, dammit, Miss Pedlar! You could become the apple of an old man's eye and end up a woman of property.'

'I'm that now,' she reminded.

'I suppose you are,' Kane temporised — 'In a sense. But I was thinking in terms of — '

'I know what you were thinking,' the girl interrupted, her expression suggesting that whatever she said next was going to hold a sting; but her flow was broken as the waitress returned with a tin tray in her hands that bore a coffee pot, two cups and saucers, a basin of sugar, two plates and a dish of buttered toast.

'Don't get the idea I'm trying to force you into a job,' Kane said, setting everything out on the tabletop and pouring for them both after the waitress had withdrawn. He indicated that Jill should help herself, then went on: 'It's all up to you, of course. But if you'd like me to speak to Henry Thompson for you, I'll gladly do it.'

'Thank you,' the blonde said, eating with signs of appetite, 'but I don't think I'm ready for this yet.'

Kane nodded his understanding. 'Just a matter of striking while the iron's hot. Few things come along and fit into life exactly as we'd like. Maybe I could persuade the old man to hold the arrangement in abeyance. It would have to be up to him, of course. Job-seekers don't make conditions, do they?'

Sighing, Jill Pedlar looked out of the window rather abstractedly and murmured, 'I guess not, Adam.' But then her upper body stiffened abruptly and she put down her toast, gazing hard as a big, grim-faced man, clad in a wide-brimmed hat and black suit, rode past the glass in a westerly direction, a display of weapons on and about him that was threatening in itself, while his huge grey horse added to the picture of discouragement created by the pair, for it had a magnificent barrel and haunches and a head which could have belonged to the sire of all warhorses.

The fixity of the blonde's stare caused Kane to concentrate on the passer-by as he would not have done in normal circumstances, and he now saw what he might otherwise have missed. 'Great balls of fire!' he exclaimed, as his briefly groping mind made contact with what it was seeking. 'It's that Yankee colonel — Alonzo Barris — the most infamous of the Union raiders behind our lines during the war. I saw him one or two places up north after the surrender. He was the guy who shot and robbed Professor James Firman over at River Park in sixty-four.'

'It's him all right,' Jill Pedlar agreed, as the horseman moved past the window on her companion's left and out of sight. 'I wonder what he's doing back here? Him and his infernal band did enough harm in these parts during the one time they came down here during the war. Barris rode up to our place and threatened to kill dad and me just for being southerners. Him and his men took every scrap of food we had by us. But it was what they stole from the professor that really mattered. Jim Firman called it 'The Treasure of the Lone Star'. It was made up of all the jewels and such that he'd brought back from his expeditions to the lost cities and burial grounds down in Mexico. A hundred precious objects from the Aztec day that were to have been sold off to fund the Confederate cause. They might have brought in a million dollars. It could have made all the difference to how the war was going just then.'

'I doubt it,' Kane said heavily. 'We were beaten before that piece of marauding. And we can't blame Barris too much. It was his job. He was no worse, if as bad, as Quantrell and Bill Anderson. If blame there's to be, it must fall on the blabber-mouths down here who talked so damn loud about what Jim Firman intended to do with that so-called treasure of his that the Union high command got to hear of it — through its spies, I suppose — and sent Colonel Barris and those uniformed brigands of his to steal it for them.' He smiled sardonically at the tabletop before him. 'Not that any of it did them much good, did it? As I heard the story, after the colonel had grabbed the jewels and such, he sent the bulk of his raiding party off to the south — with the treasure in their keeping — because he'd heard that a troop of Confederate cavalry was hunting him to the north of River Park. In order to draw our boys off the main body of Yankees, he rode right straight across the path of our cavalry, while the men he was aiming to save headed into the swamps near your home and got bogged down in the third arm of the mire, which is the most treacherous one of the three that make up Pedlar's Claw. As one lot of men sank from sight, those trying to rescue them went down too, and finally all were lost and the Aztec treasures with them. To round all this off, our horse soldiers caught up with Alonzo Barris and his handful of diversionary riders. They killed the Yankees almost to a man. The colonel and his sergeant major were the only two raiders to get away, and I heard the sergeant major was killed later on in the war.'

The girl shifted on her chair, and Kane sensed a waning interest in her. Her face was blank and her lower lip was trapped between her teeth. She was an uneasy figure, and Kane wondered why he should be picking up a sense of apprehension from her. But then she said, as if trying to deny that half her mind was functioning elsewhere: 'Yes, the Yankees had their doubts as to whether the colonel and Sergeant Major Amos Sweeting returned to their lines with the whole truth of what had happened in Puchero County, but — '

'Indeed,' Kane acknowledged, picking up the thread again as she dropped it. 'With such wealth involved — and such a total disaster occurring after its theft — they suspected there could be jiggery-pokery involved; but almost anything can happen in war and, as the treasure didn't benefit the Confederate cause, the whole affair was soon passed over and it's hardly been mentioned since. More important events came along to put it out of peoples' minds. I think it's generally accepted today that Professor Firman's treasure is lying at the bottom of the Pedlar's Claw with the remains of the cavalrymen who were trying to take it out of Texas.' The girl nodded absently, and the sheriff began to frown. 'You all right, Jill? What's wrong?'

'I'm sorry, Adam,' she replied, 'but I must leave right away. I wasn't thinking. I shouldn't have come in here with you. The undertaker's men will be going to my house. They have to pick up dad's body, and the door is locked against them. You do understand?'

'Sure,' Kane said. 'Did the undertaker say he'd be sending his men to your home more or less straight away?'

'Sort of. He said to expect them soon.'

It was pretty weak, but plausible enough. Kane knew that he would not be justified in expressing doubt as to her motives for wishing to leave. But he felt that she was either lying or not speaking the whole truth about the undertaker's men. Intuition warned him that she had some stronger reason for what she intended here. It must have something to do with the arrival of Alonzo Barris in the district. Nor could he forget how dextrously she had smothered his attempt to get off a shot at Tony Essen. He was a sheriff, and all sheriffs were men with suspicious natures. Was he allowing his imagination to run wild? Could there be a link up between Tony and Jill that was beyond his comprehension right now? Was it possible that coincidence had indeed — as he had not questioned until this moment — covered the fact that he had on this very same morning seen not just one, or even two faces, but three that he had not seen in years? Tony represented present crime. Colonel Alonzo Barris represented a lost fortune from the past? And Jill Pedlar — ? Well, you could say that she had known them both.

The girl had risen from her chair, and was thanking him very prettily for the toast and coffee. Getting up also, Kane inclined his head politely and said they must do it again one of these days. Jill smiled, agreeing that that would be nice. Then, as she turned from him, he observed: 'The yellow dress tells me you came to town in your buggy.'

'Yes,' she answered over her shoulder. 'I left it in Emma Holloway's back yard. Goodbye, Adam.'

'Fare-you-well,' he responded, sitting down again as he watched her leave the restaurant and pass the window on his left, her hems slightly lifted as her heels tapped rapidly along the board-walk and she vanished westwards.

Kane emptied his coffee cup. Then he tried another piece of toast, but dropped it again distastefully. Now he touched the front of his skull once more. He was developing a headache, and there was pain in the bone. Perhaps he had been more hurt than he had thought. He felt jaded and out of kilter with the world and its affairs. If only he could get his mind straight as to whether or not something dubious was building nearby. There could be no denying that many strange things happened to a man in his lifetime, and that coincidence could never be ruled out, for events of a similar nature did often appear together and seem to have a significance that later proved false. Yet events did come with their own clues, and a man had to trust his instincts.

River Park had been the centre of that treasure theft during the war, and it could well be that Colonel Alonzo Barris was headed there today. The man's business might indeed prove to be his own business — and the affairs of Tony Essen and Jill Pedlar quite separate from each other and unconnected with it — but, in the final analysis, a sheriff was paid to put his nose into everybody's business and accept the consequences if he made a mess of things.

He, Adam Kane, could do without the job right now, but he felt that he must ride over to River Park — without delay.

# 3

After leaving the 'Blue Bay' restaurant a minute or two later, Kane went straight back to his office and got his horse, a chestnut gelding, out of the stables there. Then, with Jim Derby, his deputy, in attendance and listening to what he had to say, gave a rough account of the events in which he had recently been involved and outlined his suspicions concerning them. Inevitably, Derby, who was able enough in his own right, started asking questions of the probing kind, but the sheriff was not prepared to extend the précis that he had already provided by underlining this point or denying that and, having assured his helper that he would involve him fully, if and when it became necessary, he left the office ground with a salute and rode westwards out of town.

The trail was well-defined — cut deep, indeed, by coastal traffic of a vehicular nature — and he soon topped the first ridge beyond Rockford and then began trotting his mount across the brief plateau beyond it, a view of the sunken swamp-lands of the Trinity delta south of him and on the left. He could just make out the black lagoons amidst the equally black and rotten forests of the district. Down there Spanish moss cascaded and a form of grey mildew coated every growing thing in sight. Those woodlands were foul places that few people would wish to visit for themselves. There the watersnakes danced and writhed amidst the floating alligators, and leeches clung to the weeds and vegetation rotting under the water. Drifting mists and a miasmic stench covered all, and the only resolution occurred where the nexus of death and decay debouched as fingers of dark stain into the cleansing blue floods which rolled in off the Gulf of Mexico. These were occasionally visible at the limit of sight from the highest points of land along the sheriff's route.

Most of the time, however, Kane kept his eyes on the country immediately before him. This, a tip of the great Texas plain, fell in uneven steps — often brown and stained by ocean salt — into the south, filling due west and much of the northern quadrant of his view, with the details of the lower lying distances spreading the fringes of the scene into fine perspective and bringing a sense of light and beauty to both the back of Puchero County and its middle ground.

Kane lifted his gaze fully only once or twice. It was this central terrain — land no more than three or four miles beyond him — that formed his goal and held most of his attention. Over to his right, and standing back in the shadows of the scene — splendidly framed by cypress groves and the remains of once orderly gardens — was a white mansion of the Colonial style, with its balconies, shuttered windows and Doric columns, still intact, though the sheriff knew the house to be the largely fire-gutted remains of the home that Professor James Firman, archaeologist, antiquarian, collector of relics and explorer, had occupied pre-war in national estate and fame — while over to the left, though well forward of the dark line marking off the River Park grounds, were the far less impressive but still nicely planned cottage and gardens of Ivan Pedlar who prior to his death yesterday, had been a haunter of the swamps not far to the southeast of his property and a slayer of alligators for their hides.

Nor was it the stillness of the scene that fixed Kane's attention, for movement was also visible on the wedge of land below him and ahead. A vehicle that was obviously a hearse — and no doubt the one sent out by Rockford's undertaker to pick up the mortal remains of Ivan Pedlar — was rolling along the trail that Kane was himself travelling. The vehicle was a mile or so ahead and making a turn towards the late Ivan's gate, where the horse and buggy which the deceased's daughter had used to get into town were already standing.

Well, there was no arguing with the evidence and the details of it were proof that Jill Pedlar's sudden excuse for leaving the 'Blue Bay' restaurant had been a valid one. Yet, while it came as a sort of relief to find that the blonde had not lied to him outright, Kane still believed that there had been an ulterior motive buried in the reason that she had given for her abrupt departure from town. It was possible, he supposed, that she had simply wanted to reach home ahead of her visitors — expected or potential — to make sure that nobody got into her house by force while she was not there. That seemed to imply that she had something to protect or did not want them to find. But what? She and her papa had been poor enough down

45

the years. Even so — It gave a man furiously to think!

Kane clapped on speed. He had no clear idea as to why he should be using his spurs, but there was some vague notion in his brain of overtaking the undertaker's men and reaching Jill Pedlar's home before their arrival. He asked himself, as speed made him think more lucidly, whether he could in fact be looking for an excuse himself to enter the girl's dwelling — possibly with a view to poking around like the worst of intruders — but realized that that could not be allowable in the present circumstances and then wondered if, perhaps, Jill would let him question her about the last days of her father's life and his final doings. Subconsciously, he felt that Colonel Alonzo Barris must be the hub of any irregular activities that might be threatening hereabouts, and that somebody could have invited or even summoned the Yankee back into these parts. That 'somebody' could have been Ivan —

46

A shot cracked out distantly, its echoes seeming to swell upwards in Kane's direction and spread beyond him as a harsh but fading roar. The sound came from just this side of where the northern quarter of the sheriff's vision began — or in the region of the approaches to the ruined River Park mansion — and reining back to a halt, Kane rose up in his stirrups and gazed intently towards the spot, picking out the shape of a rider among the brush. and clumped grasses of the area. Was it Barris there? Or had Barris fired on somebody? Hell, it might not even be the Yankee colonel! He, Kane, was permitting his mind to execute every kind of undisciplined trick it wished. It wouldn't do. Lack of any real detective work had made his brain lazy of late. He must obtain a more trustworthy picture of what was happening here and compel his mind to deal in facts only.

He was carrying field-glasses. They could be of the greatest help to a lawman, but he seldom used them these days — which was foolish of him. Now, however, he settled back into his saddle and unbuckled the leather bag behind his right knee, rummaging out his binoculars and putting them to his eyes, where he promptly made the adjustment necessary to bringing the images which had just now been fairly obscure into a much enhanced field of vision, and he soon satisfied himself that the rider over two miles beyond him was indeed Barris.

The Yankee was halted too. A hand upon one of the pieces of artillery that decorated his saddle, he was peering fixedly to his right. He appeared hesitant — a state of mind that Kane would never have associated with such a decisive character as he — but seemed on the verge of giving chase to a marksman that he could not in fact see and whom the sheriff certainly could not; but Barris remained in check and, after a few moments more in his halted state and uncertain frame of mind, sent his horse into a direct forward motion again. Keeping his head down, he headed for the crumbling Firman property at a spanking pace and, while the sheriff's field-glasses went on covering him, crossed the remaining ground between him and the house and halted outside it. There he sat irresolute again, and had still to dismount when, its sound far more muffled than the first, a second shot banged and Kane's ear traced the detonation to the interior of the ruins themselves. Even now Barris held his ground; then, as if somebody unseen had shouted to him from indoors, he came back to life with kicking heels and moved off southwards across the front of the old mansion at full gallop, vanishing into the black gloom of the cypress stands beyond it less than a minute later.

What the deuce was going on yonder? Kane was even more mystified than before. He had almost forgotten about Jill Palmer and her wooden home by now — the undertaker's men and their hearse too — and, after thrusting his field-glasses back into the saddle-bag, he dug his spurs into his mount's flanks and drew the chestnut's head a little to the right, going for the decaying Firman place over the shortest route available and not easing up on his horse for an instant. Shots were almost invariably fired with the intention of killing, and he had a strong hunch that somebody had just died over there in the ruined mansion.

The slope which formed the reverse ground under the plateau off which he had commenced his gallop seemed longer than Kane had expected. Minutes went by before he arrived on the flatter going lower down. His horse strode well on the middle grasses and offered no complaint as he kept prodding and lashing at it. Now the images which he had seen through his field-glasses grew magically around him and took on substance, and he felt a life that had not been evident in his lenses come upon him as a singing of birds, a cracking of the air in high branches, and the squeaking of prairie dogs frightened back into their holes on old lawns that were now no better than unkempt meadows. He could also feel a life force in the cool of the river which flowed behind the house, the smell of orchids in the joints of rotting timber, and the toss of rhododendrons not yet in flower. He knew that in this corruption of grace the splendour of the Old South lay stricken. Romance itself had perished here, and it would have eaten Kane's heart out had he been a sensitive soul, but he refused to be other than a practical man and wasted no thought on what used to be. He lived for the day, and this day was not shaping up too well.

Soon he drew rein where Alonzo Barris had stopped about a quarter of an hour before him. Then he sprang down from his saddle and, after throwing the nearby ruin the briefest of apprehensive glances, ran forward through the columns that supported

51

what was left of the crumbling mansion's east face and entered the place, all too conscious of the hollow emptiness of the rooms and corridors on every hand and the brown and smoky stains of fire which had spread their shapeless films on the ceilings and walls of his immediate surroundings. Once a man of national consequence had held court here among his peers, but his works and mission had been wiped out forever by a bullet and a few blazing brands put to drapes and furniture by a party of ignorant soldiers. Kane shook his head at the folly of it all, as he had before — since a man could be as practical and dismissive as he liked and still feel the impact of what had happened at River Park — but the greatest folly had been the war itself. It had slain the best men of their generation and bankrupted the nation. If it had settled anything at all — and Kane doubted it — the price had been incalculably too great. But you had to accept it. The one thing you'd never change was human nature, with all its greed and violence — and prating hypocrisy.

His tread a swift and light one as he passed along, the sheriff sent his eyes probing into every corner as he examined the ruin's northern end, but he saw nothing to explain the gunshot which had brought him here in such haste — and was beginning to believe that the events of the day had made him over-sensitive to minor portents — when he recalled that the decaying mansion's largest and most popular room, the meeting place of its one-time master and his friends, was at the other end of the house; for there James Firman had set up what he had called his 'museum and show place' in what had once been the mansion's ballroom, an airy, high-ceilinged annexe which had provided access to a south-facing conservatory and River Park's marble walks and rosegardens.

Turning about, Kane went straight back through the house to the heat-shattered glazing of the once magnificent annexe — where the looters of the years between had left nothing of the smallest value in place and actually dug up and removed the parquetry flooring itself — and there he saw at once that his first intuition had not been at fault, for a man lay sprawled out upon his back not far beyond the door at the inner end of the room and seemed to have recently bled out, since he was lying in a red and congealing pool that was a good five feet across it. Noting that the other had been shot dead centre, Kane didn't even bother to crouch and examine him, but stood above him instead and gave his full attention to the deceased's face, which became familiar to him after he had made allowances for the ageing process of the decade since he had last seen it. The ruddy skin around the staring eyes and sharp, thin features was distinctly ravaged — as was that wrinkled over the thickly corded neck — while temporal baldness had reduced a fine crop of red hair to a few gingery sprouts and wisps on the pink skin which it had once so thickly covered. Here lay Bradley Firman, the late professor's only son, and a man who had disappeared from Puchero County after a quarrel with his father in Eighteen sixty-two and never been spoken of since in these parts.

So mystery piled on top of mystery, and the obvious questions soon asked to be answered. Where had Bradley Firman come from? What was he doing here? Why had he been killed? And by whom? Kane had no ready explanations. In fact he had none of any kind. Except to say that Bradley Firman had either seen something that he shouldn't or done something that he shouldn't — which, going to what logic the hour possessed, suggested that his death had had a connection with the shot that had been fired outside this property a short while back and could have been aimed at Colonel Barris.

Indeed, Kane now felt inclined to take all doubt out of that one and say that it had. So, accepting that Barris had recently survived a bushwhacking, it must follow that Bradley Firman could have been responsible for the attempt on the colonel's life and been punished accordingly. The reasoning seemed sound and well within the realms of possibility, for the lawman had seen enough through his binoculars to be sure that Barris had had a friend waiting for him in the ruins when he had arrived — a friend or accomplice who had sent the Yankee galloping off post haste once trouble had reared. Maybe the second man had been hoping to get rid of Brad Firman's body in the river before the crime could be discovered. That deduction also made sense and went well enough with the rest.

The sheriff felt a tremble of movement nearby, then sensed the tiniest of changes in the light. His heart jumped, and his stomach turned; he was not alone. There was a watcher at the further end of the ruined ballroom and over at its right-hand corner. It had to be Bradley Firman's murderer standing there; the man had not gone away. Jerking his revolver, Kane sprang instinctively to his rear, then made the smallest package of himself he could as a rifle cracked and a bullet whipped at the slack of his shirt. A shape moved at the tail of the lawman's right eye. He blazed at it, lacking any chance to take aim, and his slug brought down window-glass that was already broken and then went screeching off at a tangent as it clipped a corner of brickwork beyond the pane.

The rifle flashed a second time. Kane caught his breath as the incoming bullet flicked at the skin of his left forearm and drew blood. Galvanised by the hurt, he squared round to face his would-be killer, fanning the hammer of his revolver to get as much lead into the air as possible — and he caught the briefest glimpse of a dour-looking man, with savage, deep-set eyes under thick black brows, a jaw that was too wide for his narrow forehead, a beaky snout, and an almost rindless mouth that was full of yellow and uneven teeth. The other was probably no coward, but he showed promptly that he had lived long enough to have learned that discretion was indeed the better part of valour. Flinching, as the leaden hail nipped bits off his clothing, he whirled away from his bushwhacker's corner and vanished at the run, using the angle of the house from which he had sought to kill the lawman to protect him now. His pounding footfalls echoed back from what was left of the gardens at the southern end of the decaying property, and the sounds, only too audible to the angered Kane, invited pursuit.

Jumping over Bradley Firman's corpse, the sheriff lurched and staggered obliquely to his right across the uneven base of the ripped up parquetry floor. Within moments, Kane reached the window from which he had been fired on and tried to tug it open, but the frame was still fastened and resisted him. It opened easily enough, however, after he had lifted the catch, and he sprang up to the sill and ducked through the space that he had just cleared, leaping down to the ground below and then launching himself into the chase.

He saw his quarry at once. The man was already a fair distance ahead of him and making for the dark stands of cypress trees at the southern boundary of the River Park grounds. Kane went haring after the other without much thought for the difficulties which the entangled growth on the land before him might present. This was a mistake, and he was soon made aware of it, for he found himself tripping over bits of rubble hidden by the growth, while briars and long stalks wrapped themselves around his legs and also impeded him. He kicked and cursed, but this did not help his progress, for things got worse the further he went. This now semi-wild garden had become overgrown to the extent in some places that fish ponds, terraces and rockeries, had been obscured, and the time taken to round them — on their sudden appearances underfoot — slowed the sheriff up by half.

Kane struggled on, conscious that his quarry must be finding it a battle too. The dark man paused and fired a shot at him on one occasion, and he triggered in reply, but found that his Colt was empty and knew that this was no time to pause and reload even a chamber or two in his gun. Thrusting the weapon away, he redoubled his efforts to close the gap on the man ahead, but nothing helped very much. It occurred to him that he had expended more energy in frustration than effort, and that his body was beginning to hurt from the scratches and bruises that it had accumulated in recent moments. Add to these minor pains the headache that the glancing blow from Tony Essen's gun barrel had given him and everything about him seemed on the ebb.

He wavered, his concentration momentarily lost, then found himself in an area of sagging marble arches and toppled Grecian statues. Hesitating further, it took him seconds more to find a way out of what seemed like a maze of stone and, when he did clear it, he saw that he had reached the limit of the River Park gardens and realized that he was the clear loser of the chase. His quarry had already disappeared into the cypress stands ahead, and he had no idea of what direction the other had taken among the soaring trunks of the vast conifers.

The sense of defeat brought him to a halt. Placing his hands upon his hips, he stood there and gasped for breath. Then the sound of a galloping horse reached him from the heart of the timber. The sheriff let his chin fall; it would be useless following. He didn't doubt that the man he'd been pursuing was virtually clear and away.

Further pursuit of the immediate kind was really out of the question. Even if he pelted round to the front of the ruined house and mounted his horse instantly, lining up a hunt on horseback — with the timber blocking out all vision in between — would be a nearly impossible exercise, and searching for sign beyond the trees could prove almost as bad. However you worked it out, the time element involved would give the escaper the chance to put miles between them before the sheriff could begin chasing to a plan that might have some hope of eventually running his quarry down.

So was he to give up on it — merely ride back to Rockford and write a factual report for the county sheriff on what had happened here? It was all that was actually required of him. He was only a town sheriff and had no power outside his own bailiwick. Yes, in this case the easiest way was also the correct way. But it surely went against the grain — because, aside from so much else, he was still mad at that dark, sullen-looking man with all the teeth who had apparently murdered Bradley Firman and then tried to get the sheriff too.

# 4

Kane gave himself time to fully recover from his latest exertions. After that he moved away to his left and almost ambled around the south and forward edges of the overgrown garden as he returned to the place in front of the ruined house where he had left his horse. His mind would not give up on the question of his responsibilities in the matters that had lately involved him, and he was troubled by how fragmented his day's work seemed to have become. He ought to be able to pull things together and do more about them than appeared the case. Happenings had splurged in response to his earlier broad reasoning and seemed packed with possibilities, but now it had all shrunk together again and left him with no lead that had any feeling of purpose at the end of it. The killing here had, now that he came to place it exactly, occurred outside his area of responsibility and, though he had found a possible explanation for it, there were many others that might fit the case and could be much nearer to the truth. He felt worn out and mentally flattened. Perhaps he would ride to Jill Pedlar's house and seek that talk with her about her recently dead father's last activities. No — forget it! This business, whatever its local ramifications, really did belong with Phil Blatson, the county sheriff.

After spinning out and reloading his gun, Kane mounted up and gave his legs a stretch against the stirrup leathers. It was time to go home; he was his own master when all was said and done. So long as he kept order in Rockford, the great majority of folk around here would be satisfied with him. He wasn't qualified to play the riding marshal, and would soon be told so if he tried it. Nor was he paid enough to take the major risks that were always involved when systematically tracking down murderers and the worst kinds of criminals. He must accept himself for the lowly type of lawman that he was — bear in mind that this was a wicked world — and acknowledge that neither he nor anybody else would ever cure a tithe of the crime around. That was how to stay alive and keep his sanity. 'Come on horse,' he said aloud to his mount, drawing at its mouth with his left hand, 'let's climb yonder hill and go back home. Then we can tell the undertaker about the dead man lying here.'

The horse snorted its approval and began turning. But then Kane looked up and checked both his pull and its movement. Hundreds of seabirds had just risen into the sky beyond the nearby cypress trees and were now spreading and climbing in the kind of unison which suggested that they had been startled out of a feeding process on the land below. Kane's experience told him that a rider had just galloped up on that flock of foraging gulls and sent it soaring. The killer from this place? Could be — though it was by no means certain. If it was so, the fellow must be drifting eastwards — rather than in the opposite direction, which the sheriff had tended to be taking for granted — and this somehow made Kane's latest deduction seem less feasible to him. The man could not be a fool; he would have a clear idea of what he was doing in this district; and he must be aware that drifting eastwards could only take him deeper into the bailiwick of the one lawman that he had as yet to fear in Puchero County. Besides, where could the guy be headed on that course between the pleasant hinterland nearby and a shoreline which, with its swamps and quicksands, was often so much less?

If rider there was, could the swamps themselves be his goal? Yes, he might well be headed there, and it could be that he had sent Colonel Barris in that direction after firing the shot that had slain Bradley Firman. The culminating point in the story of the treasure of the Lone Star had been its loss in the swamps of Pedlar's Claw, and it could even be that the pair had been contemplating the recovery of the jewels from the morass this very day. But how was that to be done? Unless the treasure had never actually been swallowed up by the swamp in the first place and had in fact been hidden up over there all these years; for it seemed to Kane that he already knew enough to be sure that something more than the foundering of a military operation had occurred when Barris's command had been wiped out by the mire and the Aztec jewels involved seemingly lost to everybody.

The matter remained complex and, if it had a true existence, there were many details concerning it that needed explaining, but this could only come about if he resumed the chase and caught up with the action. Fine — but, when all was said and done — and he kept coming back to it — he couldn't be sure that the picture provided by his imagination was not entirely false and that the upsurge of the seabirds hadn't been caused by something quite different from what he had allowed his mind to suggest. The sudden appearance of a cat or dog near the feeding ground could have been enough to have brought about that eruption of the gulls. An obstinacy that more or less countered his will set in. The swamps of Pedlar's Claw were dangerous to enter, and it would be madness to move into them unless he could be certain that he had a good reason for so doing. But did he? Once more he couldn't make up his mind, and his resolve was wavering. He didn't *have* to do anything.

Then the thing which had happened before repeated. A mass of birds went rocketing upwards into the field of cloudless blue above and broke up and spread in the same fashion as before. Yet this manifestation had nothing to do with the first one, for the flock of seagulls here had risen off the ground well forward and to the left of that evacuated earlier and a good deal closer to the sea. It was possible to trace the route in the mind's-eye, and it was pretty well certain now that a rider was moving away from this area under the land and heading in the direction of the swamps known as Pedlar's Claw. It was almost bound to be Bradley Firman's killer travelling there, and the man was far enough into the Rockford bailiwick to make the responsibility for apprehending him Kane's own. The only action he could take in good conscience now would to be to go after the other. So that much was settled for him anyhow.

Kane pointed his horse just to the left of the cypress trees. Kneeing the animal into motion, he sent it cantering up the slight gradient ahead of him and soon topped out where the land turned down towards the sea. Meadows that were alight with redhot pokers, blue bonnet, pink daisies and goldenrod, rolled away from his gaze, and he received the impression that locusts were about in considerable swarms, which explained why so many gulls had flown inland. But the reason for this aerial migration off the Gulf was of little interest to him then, for the sheriff's eyes went almost at once to the bottom left-hand corner of the grassland, where a horseman was just leaving his easy traverse of the meadows for the relatively dangerous descent of the flood-damaged terraces which stepped down into the salt-browned reedlands and smooth black mudflats that adjoined the mildewed jungle of the swamps proper, where mangroves sprawled among water oaks, decaying evergreens, and a variety of choking, broad-leafed undergrowth that was veiled by streamers of Spanish moss.

Fearing that the man beyond him would crane round and see him perched atop the ridge, the sheriff held back with his horse in check; but the difficulties of riding were enough to keep the other fully occupied as he entered

71

the marsh-lands. Kane watched the horseman complete his descent and move forward onto ground that was lower still; then, feeling sure that he was judging it aright, he launched into the grassland before him and galloped in the direction of the terraces close to the sea, believing that he was riding below any level of vision which his quarry could achieve should the man look round and up while crossing the sunken reedlands along the edge of the sub-tropical morass a little further to the east.

The sheriff reined down to a slow trot on nearing the stepped descent to the marshes. He saw now that it would be distinctly to his advantage if he let the rider ahead of him pass into the Pedlar's Claw vegetation before he, Kane, guided his mount down to sea level. The other man's vision, from inside the swamp area, should be so reduced by the amount of growth around him that the likelihood of his glancing back and detecting a follower through some chink in the jungle could be virtually discounted. Anyway, whatever his recent alarms might have been, the man yonder showed no sign that he feared the possibility that he was being pursued, and his posture and movements were even a trifle reckless. He was full of purpose and not a little haste. He knew where he was going, and was plainly in a hurry to get there. If the indications were to be trusted, he would not be hanging around on the off-chance of being followed.

Stopping his horse a few yards short of the irregular steps which marked the deepest inroads of the winter seas behind the salt marshes, Kane dismounted and hunkered down in the grass beside the animal, watching his quarry's final progress and disappearance into the swamplands. Even at the last the man remained indifferent to his wake and the tracks that he had left there, and the sheriff was not the least afraid to straighten up almost at once and resume following him. Doing what he deemed the sensible thing, Kane caught his horse at the mouth and helped it down the terraces, only returning to his saddle when he reached the sand and shingle that fringed the mud below, then — keeping to the hoof-marks of the last animal which had crossed here and those of another just prior to it, Colonel Barris's great warhorse presumably — he made his own way over to the western limit of the swamps and entered there, holding to the same guidance as before, since the underfoot, though remaining firm enough just here, was also sufficiently damp at the surface to carry shoemarks that were discernible without straining the eyes; and so it went on for two hundred yards or more, when Kane slowed his horse almost to a halt on hearing a low whistle from human lips not far away that was answered within minutes by a similar one from a short distance beyond it.

The atmosphere about the sheriff

grew vaporous and sweaty. It held a tension which matched Kane's own. The black rot of the morass was everywhere to be seen, while its ugliest corners plopped and stank, warning through the total lack of life around them that they were not to be approached. Wiping off his brow, the sheriff breathed deeply to reduce the agitation of his nerves. After that he halted his horse completely and stepped quietly to the ground. Listening ahead, he waited to hear another whistle, but only the distant bark of an alligator and the noise of the birds in the ceiling of the swamp came to him. Apparently the one exchange of signals had been enough.

Kane inched forward, breathing silence as he drew his horse along beside him. Voices spoke, exchanging words that were gruff and unintelligible. There were two men all right, and he estimated that he was now within thirty yards of them. Still employing the utmost caution, he kept closing on the pair, quite certain that they would gun him down without a qualm if he showed himself prematurely. He drew his own gun and pointed it squarely ahead of him. He must protect himself, but he would only shoot if he absolutely had to, since he had questions for the pair ahead which perhaps they alone could answer.

The vegetation of the area opened a little. Kane now saw two men directly before him. They were Colonel Barris and the dour-looking man from the River Park ruin who had attempted to bushwhack the lawman not so long ago. The pair were standing beneath an oak tree which had probably been grey and dead for a generation and not far from the edge of an extensive quagmire that stretched away into greener parts of the swamp. The two men looked taut and angry, even baffled and frustrated — though not with or by each other — and they were deep in the kind of concentrated thought which only found expression in odd phrases that were terse and to the point. The sheriff was aware of the slight sounds made by his horse and himself, but the two men opposite were so immersed in their own business that they appeared to hear nothing and jumped visibly when he snapped: 'Get your hands up, the pair of you! You're my prisoners!'

'Prisoners?' Colonel Barris echoed, square-shouldered and arrogant, a towering man who was more outraged than startled. 'Who the devil are you?'

'The law in this neighbourhood,' Kane responded. 'Adam Kane, sheriff of Rockford, Colonel Barris.'

'The local sheriff, eh?' the big Yankee said. 'Do I know you?'

'Doubt not,' Kane answered. 'But I did see you up north. It was around the end of the war. You were putting on a strut with those polecats of yours. I know plenty about you, and fancy I know the reason why you're here, Colonel.'

'Fancy is right,' Barris agreed, his

mouth working in a manner which suggested that he had just tasted something uncommonly nasty.

'I think you're here to recover the Firman jewels,' Kane persisted. 'I know the story.'

'You and a million other people,' the colonel said. 'If you know the story then you must be aware that those Aztec jewels will never be recovered. The treasure of the Lone Star is lying at the bottom of this swamp.'

'I don't think it ever went into the swamp,' Kane returned boldly, fixing his eyes on the big man's dark companion. 'I believe you're Amos Sweetman, mister, the colonel's troop sergeant major. Well?'

The dark man went for his gun, but Kane fired instantly, putting a groove across the back of the other's right hand as his fingers closed on the butt of his Colt, and he cried out in pain and his saturnine visage seemed to screw up into the shape of an aged walnut as he doubled forward and held his wound tightly to reduce his suffering from it and the scarlet spillage from the torn tissues involved, 'God damn your soul, Kane!' he gritted out, subsiding against the trunk of the dead oak tree and remaining propped there.

'He'll more likely damn yours!' Kane replied unfeelingly. 'I can't think why I didn't kill you. You came close enough to doing me in not an hour ago!'

'Prove it!' the dark man snarled.

'Prove any of it, you undisciplined lout!' Colonel Barris challenged.

'You think like a lawyer,' Kane remarked. 'I daresay it'll prove itself before all is done. I figure the pattern is there, Colonel, and that alone should bring everything out in due course. For the rest, sir, you're bound to seek enough rope to hang yourselves. And, up to a point, I aim to let you have it. So be careful what you do next!'

'Don't presume to advise me, you country oaf!' Barris countered. 'Are you all right, Sweetman?'

'Yes, sir,' the dark man said thinly.

'So I was right,' Kane said with satisfaction — 'you are Amos Sweetman.'

'What's it to you, lawman?'

'I like to know a fellow's name before I drop him into eternity,' Kane answered. 'You Yankees have kept our local administration poor in these parts, and the sheriff has to do the hangman's job too. So get a good look at my face, Sweetman. It will probably be the last one you see in this world!'

'Hold your row, you croaking vulture!' Sweetman yelled, to that extent recovered from the initial pain of his injury.

'I'm building up a nice catalogue of insulting names,' Kane reflected. 'Well, sticks and stones, eh?'

'You started the name-calling,' Colonel Barris reminded.

'You and your raiders were polecats,' Kane affirmed. 'You raped the South.'

'It was war,' Barris said dismissively. 'Terrible things were done by both armies. All of it, Sheriff, is now long ago and far away. You would do well to remember that. Remember it — and let me and my companion go on our way. We are travellers — sightseers, if you like — and we have as much right in this swamp as anybody in the country. Even you.'

'That yarn is as much a lie,' Kane said, 'as the story put about that Sweetman died in one of the war's later battles. Whatever the efforts you made to get those Aztec jewels to your high command, Colonel — or seemed to make — I'd stake my all that you and Sweetman already had a plan to set aside that treasure for yourselves from the first. I'll swear you've been waiting for the years to pass — with the intention of returning here to recover the jewels when folk have forgotten everything concerning them. Figures, too, that there was a third man involved. Almost certainly, on the shape and logic of the thing, your second-in-command. I wonder if he's still alive or dead?'

'It's a matter of military record,' the colonel said, not above sounding superior after the fashion of men whom he would have deemed lesser ones, 'that Major Samuel Riggs died the day the treasure was lost — and in this same swamp.' He uttered a scoffing laugh. 'You think you know so much. In fact you know nothing.'

'In saying what you just said,' Kane reminded, 'you admitted that there is something to know.'

'Words,' Barris said, letting a forefinger spiral upwards — 'just words.'

'No witnesses either,' Sweetman sneered, straightening off the dead tree again and wrapping a dirty handkerchief around his still profusely bleeding hand. 'Why don't you do what the colonel suggested, lawman? Let him and me go. You ain't hurt — but I am. You've nothing on us. No harm's been done. Right?'

'Wrong,' Kane retorted. 'Had you forgotten Bradley Firman is dead? You shot him, Sweetman! Do I have to remind you again of what happens to murderers in Puchero County?'

'You braying ass!'

'Keep it up, boys!' Kane encouraged ironically.

'You will show me a proper respect!' the colonel barked out.

'Or you'll what?' Kane inquired, spitting out his own contempt. 'We're not playing at soldiers now, Barris. You've done wrong where I say what goes. I have a body back at River Park, and I'm holding both of you.'

'What's the charge?' Barris demanded. 'Be specific, man!'

'Should be obvious, Colonel,' Kane replied. 'Suspicion of murder.'

'I did no more than ride past that ruined house,' the big Yankee said.

'That's not quite how I saw it,' the sheriff retorted.

'You saw it?'

'Through my field-glasses, yes,' Kane explained. 'I was sitting high, to the east of here, and watching you ride onto the Firman estate. You stopped outside the River Park ruin, Colonel, and didn't ride on until Sweetman — who seems to have been your shadow and protector — called to you from indoors so to do. Sure, there's a speculative element about it — but, putting it with the rest of the evidence, it should be enough to justify holding you behind bars for the next twenty-four hours.'

'This is beyond belief!' Barris declared, setting his hands upon his hips and glowering into the sheriff's face.

'Do be careful,' Kane warned. 'Amos Sweetman was of a similar frame of mind — and look what happened to him.'

'Pshaw!'

'I want you to unlatch your gunbelts and let them fall,' the sheriff said. 'Easy about it now! You're old soldiers, and not this new breed of fast guns.'

Barris and Sweetman did as commanded. Their gunbelts fell dully to the ground. Now Kane gestured for the pair to kick their belts towards him. This the pair did also. Then the sheriff picked the leatherwork up and cast it and the Colts holstered thereupon over the shoulders of his mount. After that he said: 'You first, Colonel. Go to your horse. You have a shotgun on it big enough to sink a man-o'-war, and a rifle too. Unbuckle them from your nag, sir, and throw them into the undergrowth yonder. When he's done, Sweetman, you do the same. Got it?'

Once more the prisoners did as they had been ordered, though the colonel's angry complaints about the value of his weapons must have been audible at the further side of the swamp. 'You'll never see a better bear gun than that!' he declared finally, as he threw his great shotgun into the bushes.

'Eight to the barrel,' Sweetman agreed subserviently. 'Can settle the hash of the biggest bruin that ever was!'

'Well, we don't have bears around here,' Kane assured them, 'and I'd surely hate to see what that cannon could do to a man.'

'You'll hear more of it, Kane!' Barris promised bitterly.

'That's right,' the sheriff approved, 'you tell Lawyer Higgins. Now bring your horses over here, gents, and let's get out of this stinking place.'

The colonel and Sweetman walked their mounts over to join Kane, and he kept them under the muzzle of his revolver every yard of the way. He had just decided that it should be safe to let them ride out of the swamp ahead of him — and was getting ready to tell them to mount up and move off at the slowest of paces — when a man came reeling out of the vegetation on the right of the exit path and other figures stepped into view at his back, the biggest of these, a fellow well over six-feet tall and of a devil-may-care cut of jib, waving two revolvers and grinning crookedly as he proclaimed: 'It's Cap'n Jack Starbuck and company, friends! Kindly stay where you are!' He let fly with a brutal kick at the buttocks of the man on his side — Tony Essen — who had first appeared from the swamp greenery, the force of his boot's arrival no doubt explaining Tony's earlier reeling motion at the instant of his bursting into the open. 'I have some questions to ask!' Starbuck concluded, kicking again to such purpose that he propelled Essen off his feet and onto his face.

Questions, eh? It seemed that damned nigh everybody had questions to ask. And Kane could guess about what. Those Aztec jewels were becoming *the* most desirable property and the toast of the day. But how in tarnation blazes had Jack Starbuck found his way into this business?

Kane let his revolver fall as he saw how many pistols were covering him. It was not just Alonzo Barris and Amos Sweetman who were in trouble now. So was he.

# 5

Looking closely at Tony Essen's features, as the young man pressed his upper body off the ground by using the strength of his arms and hands, Kane saw the marks of brutal punishment present, and he got the impression that Essen had been well and truly beaten up at a distance from this spot before being brought here. It figured, then, that Tony had misbehaved in some way that had outraged his boss and fellow outlaws. There had clearly been a great deal in the lead up to what was taking place here that Kane did not know enough about as yet to even start comprehending, which meant of course that he could only look on and hope that matters would become clearer to him as these latest events developed.

There was certainly a lot of energy going into the sheer savagery of it.

Kane was not a squeamish man. In his job he could not afford to be. He had seen plenty of cruelty in his time, but he nevertheless winced as Jack Starbuck sprang at the rising Tony and flattened him again by ramming a heel against the back of his head and then holding his face in the dirt. After that, to the sheriff's further disapproval, the lean but perfectly built gang-boss thrust his revolvers away and seized his victim by the belt and scruff of the neck, lifting him bodily and swinging him to the front, where he dropped him just short of the dead oak tree and yelled: 'Is this the tree you told us about, you traitorous houndawg?'

Essen was obviously almost too dazed to speak, but Starbuck stamped on the middle of his back and hectored: 'Is it? Well — is it?'

'Gotta be, Jack,' Essen wailed. 'Gotta be?'

'Gotta be,' Starbuck mimicked. 'How so?'

'It's the one Ivan Pedlar described

to me,' Essen answered, 'and that doggone sheriff and — and the other two bastards are here, ain't they?'

'And that proves it?' Starbuck hectored anew. 'Will you stake your life this is the tree, Tony?'

'Look for yourself,' Essen insisted. 'There's no other one around like it. It's dead, and grey, and its roots are out of the ground — and what's left of its branches are thrown into the air like the arms of a screamin' woman. Can you see another one around here that even looks like it?'

'A nice how d'you do altogether!' Starbuck proclaimed disgustedly. 'It's a real good job I got suspicious and began keeping an eye on you, Tony. You and that girlfriend you kept telling me you had to keep riding out to see. If I hadn't followed you and found you out, you'd have gotten away with a fortune here — and never a piece of gold for me and your pals. Oh, you rat, you skunk, you toad! It's always been my rule — since we went to the bad after the war — share and share alike. And there's you riding over Rockford way and trying to pull this one on me. A fortune, blast your eyes — a goldurned, copper-bottomed fortune — and you were out to hang on to the lot! I ought to stamp your brains out, mister!' He raised his head, fighting for breath and words. 'Even now I don't know the half of it, I'll lay.'

'You do, Jack!' Essen wailed, his voice still begging for mercy. 'You do! It ain't as terrible as you make out!' He stirred, and was stamped on again. 'Ouch! You speak of the lot, Jack. I wasn't going to get the lot — or even a big piece of it. I've told you how it was — and is. Them jewels are only a fortune if they can be turned into spending money. That was why Ivan Pedlar asked help of me and I, in my turn, hunted up Bradley Firman. You've got to have the right contacts up north for selling off treasures and such. Bradley Firman had them. Hell,

Jack, be fair! How was I to know Firman would do the dirty on me and make contact with his old partner in crime, Colonel Barris? Any more than I could know the colonel would then send for that stinking, lowborn side-kick of his, Amos Sweetman. Little of it was intended, but much has grown.'

'Firman only summoned Barris to River Park,' Starbuck announced, eyeing the colonel vindictively, 'so that you could bushwhack him. And well you know it, you consarned liar! Barris would never have allowed Firman to sell off those jewels and keep any part of the proceeds. There's a grapevine up there — and how! They're top-drawer people, and live in the world of top-drawer folk. It all goes round in their society, and real secrets are few. I learned that when I rose from the ranks to my captaincy during the war. Those high-born folk live in a shiny world of their own above the rest of us.' He considered the big Yankee with rather less venom now.

'It figures the colonel didn't quite trust what was happening down here, though. Suspected something, didn't you, mister?'

Facing about, Barris displayed hands locked over his tailbone that flapped at Captain Starbuck in a kind of detached disdain.

'Yes, you did, Colonel,' Starbuck insisted. 'That's why you called that evil shadow of yours out of retirement to watch your back down south. It's all part of the past anyhow. From what I've beaten out of Tony Essen, that he got from Ivan Pedlar — who was hidden up in this swamp that day and saw your second-in-command, Major Riggs, send your raiders into the mire — it had all been planned with obvious care and nobody involved, least of all you, Colonel, can escape their guilt. No sooner were your troopers struggling in the mire, Barris, than Major Biggs, the man you'd put in charge, withdrew from the scene and hid the loot from the Firman estate under that dead oak tree. No doubt he was about to ride for it and rejoin that diversionary party of yours somewhere up country when, by a real trick of fate, he rode into a boghole himself and that was the end of him too. It was likewise the end of your plan to get rich from — '

Moving abruptly, Colonel Barris swung back to face Starbuck again and his expression told that he no longer had any intention of trying to remain aloof from the story being told or deny anything concerning it. 'Very well, mister,' he said in his sharpest military tones. 'You've just explained a good deal for me. But knowing all this, sir, why the devil are you here and acting like a searcher? Those Aztec baubles aren't where you say they were hidden and can't have been for years.'

'Oh, but you're wrong, Colonel!' Starbuck retorted. 'It wouldn't be wrong to say this business has some curious angles to it. Ivan Pedlar was never anybody's hero; in fact he was damn poor stuff. He was too scared by all that he had witnessed to risk taking anything away from the hiding place. He peeped in, sure enough, to find out what was there, and I suspect that, seeing straight off that the loot wasn't in coin and something pretty much outside his understanding, he just let it lie for years after as his secret. Indeed, it wasn't until he realized that he was dying — and wanted to make some sort of provision for his daughter — that he finally turned his mind to considering if there wasn't some means by which he could turn the treasure into money. That was when Tony Essen, who'd long been haunting the Pedlar property like a lovesick porcupine, came into it. And you've already heard what he had to say about Bradley Firman and the rest of it.'

'Yes, I heard,' the colonel acknowledged. 'But you need to amend your theory, Starbuck, as to why Firman had that attempt made to bush-whack me. You should get your ideas straight, Captain. There's no wonderful world at the top of society, you know. Allowing for the obvious difference that money and position make, the basic experiences of life aren't so different for any of us. Bradley Firman wanted to engineer my death because I knew that it was he who had betrayed to the Union high command his father's intention of selling off the treasure of the Lone Star as a boost to the finances of the Confederacy. A few public words from me concerning that particular piece of treachery and Bradley Firman would never have been allowed to enjoy the proceeds of his crimes by ex-friends or enemies alike. Nobody can abide a man who betrays his father in the hope of benefitting from his father's enemies. That's aside from the simple question of what the law might do.'

'Well, there,' Starbuck said indifferently, though appearing edified nevertheless, 'ain't that the truth though? But you didn't have to spill it, Colonel. It makes no difference to anything. You're a dead man — and I suspect that you already know it. Goes for Sweetman too. The pair of you are neither use nor ornament. I'm going to shoot the both of you — then into the swamp you go. It's only fitting that the colonel should rot with the rest of his command at the bottom of the bog. Justice, too, for the Confederacy you violated so often.'

'As if it mattered to you, Starbuck!' Barris literally yawned. 'You're not going to kill me, and I'll tell you why.'

'Do tell,' Starbuck encouraged, sending a grin among his companions which said this was going to be worth hearing. 'But don't try to sell me a bill-of-goods, sir. I won't be deceived by you.'

'It's plain as the nose on your face,' Barris responded. 'How can you miss the obvious, man? Are you really so different from that man Pedlar? What arrangements have you in hand to dispose of the treasure?'

Starbuck looked oddly disconcerted,

but he didn't say anything.

'Exactly,' the colonel said. 'You have no plan. Those jewels will be of no more worth to you than they were to Ivan Pedlar. They do indeed have to be reduced to cash before they benefit any of you. I, in conjunction with Bradley Firman, had already set up a chain of dealers and jewelsmiths to dispose of the treasure before coming here. You could be looking at a million dollars, Captain, but you won't see a penny of it without me. I'm worth a whole lot more to you alive than dead. The only person you need kill here is that fool of a sheriff.'

Starbuck had lowered his face thoughtfully. 'I guess you do have the right of me there, Barris,' he admitted. 'A million dollars, hey? As much as that!' He whistled long and thinly, eyeing his followers again. 'You know, boys, a man can forget a lot of principles for a sum like that. Perhaps this Yankee colonel isn't such a bad fellow after all.'

'In me, Captain, you see yourself,' Barris said with dignity. 'We're two of a kind.'

'Well, now,' Starbuck remarked comfortably, 'I can live with that. However, there is a slight problem. I think you may have been supposing, Colonel, that I either have the loot or know where it is. I don't. If it isn't under that dead tree — and I have to assume that it isn't, since I reckon you'd have fished it out before now and have it in plain sight — I don't know where it is.'

'I can't help you,' Tony Essen bleated.

'Oh, come!' Barris urged. 'It is a problem, yes, but it can't be that perplexing.'

'Not perplexin' at all,' Sweetman put in. 'Heck, there's only one place the jewels can be, if they ain't here, and that's on the Pedlar property. I mean, whatever other sense can you make of it? Pedlar must at last have got

99

brave and fished 'em out from under the tree.'

'Finally took 'em home,' Starbuck agreed. 'Yea or nay, Tony?'

'Ivan didn't say a word to me about it,' Essen answered. 'But Sweetman must be right. It's the only sense you can make of it. If the stuff ain't here, it's just bound to be there. In Ivan's cottage.'

'It all rests with the girl now,' Sweetman said. 'You'll have to speak to her real sharp, Captain Starbuck. Maybe sting her up some, eh?'

'You don't have to lay into Jilly about this!' Tony Essen declared, sounding panicky as his tongue rubbered around his bruised mouth. 'She don't know a word about any of it. Her daddy didn't want her to be worried.'

'Be your age, son,' Sweetman advised sighing. 'What would she be likely to tell you? What did men ever know about women? The gals have been keepin' their own counsel and deceiving their menfolk ever since Eve got into the business. Ain't that right, Colonel?'

'Quiet, Sweetman!' Barris ordered. 'It's an irrelevance. The captain will know how to take the girl's house apart if he has to.'

'I will that,' Starbuck assured them all, yet with a hint of reluctance in his tones. 'I do what I have to do — always — but I'm not keen on roughing up women. Too often makes enemies where you had friends before.'

'Do you have any friends?' the colonel asked insidiously. 'Do you need any friends?'

All eyes were on Starbuck — including Kane's — but he was the one least interested in the captain's expected denial of weakness, since he was now the only man present who was at risk of being slain very shortly and cast into the nearby morass. He had for several minutes been praying for half a chance to make a break for it — as such an opportunity could well mean the difference between life and death for him — and he believed that he had been granted his half chance now, for it seemed that at this moment everybody had lost sight of his presence. So, screwing himself up in every possible way, he spun round and dived past the dead oak tree, heading into the swamp beyond and making for the densest of its vegetation.

He was only a few yards clear of Starbuck and the rest of them, when his escape registered with two or three of the outlaws who had been facing him and a cry of alarm rang out. Then bullets began to fly and the morass dinned with the echo of gunfire, birds rocketing all over the place and basking alligators in the lagoons sending up bubbles as they dived for the safety of the murky depths in which they lived.

Gritting his teeth, Kane tipped back his head and kept pumping his arms, driving himself east-wards with every scrap of energy that he could summon and, knowing the risk of falling into a boghole himself if he deviated from the obviously solid ground on which the largest of the timber in the locality grew, tried to stay in line with the biggest of the trees while zig zagging as much as he dared. Bullets zipped and whimpered within inches of him, and he expected his light to go out at any instant, but he remained unscathed as the distance between him and the guns lengthened and the tightness in his brain relaxed a little as green cover of the bush variety began to spring up around him in glades well beyond the larger and more open features at his starting point.

Presently the shooting virtually ceased, but that did not mean that the men at Kane's back had given up their intention to bring him down. He could hear the splash and trample of their feet as they started to pursue him, and felt the sharpness of their voices as they called advice to one another. He estimated that he had gained a lead of more than a hundred yards on the nearest of his hunters, but judged that his foes were no longer sure of his position on the ground ahead of them, which meant that he had room in which to manoeuvre; so, still shunning any drift towards the really dangerous lagoons and morasses on his right, the sheriff shifted his line of travel and began angling northwards. He stayed on this slowly tightening course for around five minutes, his ears telling him almost from the first that his pursuers — who ought to have anticipated his craft on the lie of the land alone — had become confused and were running straight onwards. It seemed that they had lost him where the hazards to their own safety were so numerous that the concentration they had to expend on watching where they set their feet down soon outgrew the attention they could give to seeking him. Eventually he could hear no human sound rising from the swamp behind him and felt that, barring accidents, his escape was complete for the moment.

With sweat streaming down his face and the lungs burning in his chest,

Kane reeled to a halt in the middle of a birch stand and flung his arm around a slender tree, hanging there bent at the waist as he panted for breath. That had been about the narrowest squeak of his life, and he doubted that he would have survived it once in ten times. This must be one of his luckier days, if you discounted the number of things that had already gone wrong and could have got him killed off, and he couldn't help wondering what might still be in store for him. His situation remained parlous enough, heaven knew!

Lifting his head, Kane gazed about him. He had never felt more isolated and alone. What was he going to do next? It would be madness to stay in this area where his enemies were now so numerous and would soon be deploying to get him at all costs, but he had been forced to abandon his horse back there and had only his two feet left to him. What chance did a man afoot have against mounted hunters? He was up against some of the devil's best, and their power to think things out was at least the equal of his own. They would realize that his aim would be to get back to Rockford and form a posse, and that that would mean crossing miles of open ground where he could be spotted and overtaken with ease. If he did what they expected, he would be almost literally at their mercy — especially as he was also now unarmed — but, short of circling miles out of his way, he couldn't see anything for it but to attempt what his foes would anticipate.

He began moving onwards, his brain working overtime as he jogged through the trees. There'd got to be some means of getting through this. He couldn't let a seeming inevitability drive him to his death. It would be better to go into hiding than that. Colonel Barris and Jack Starbuck would only seek him for so long. Part of what had become their joint force would be seeking the Aztec jewels on the Pedlar property while the rest would be hunting for him. Once the jewels had been located, the badmen might decide to waste no further time on him and get out of the district fast. That could be greatly to his advantage too. For the question of his limited responsibility, as a town sheriff, would immediately raise itself again, and he could then — as he had observed to himself not so long ago — turn the whole business over to the county sheriff without any bending of the rules. But once more he had to ask himself whether he wanted the easy way out. He was a stubborn man, and had set his hand to the plough. He would feel at least demeaned if he had to turn back. Besides, if he gave up now, the robbers might never be caught and he would hate to have his name associated with one of the biggest thefts that the United States had ever seen. He would reach Rockford somehow, and without pausing further. He needed a horse, and he would get one, beg, borrow — or steal. The day had not been without its minor miracles, and where could be the harm in looking for another one?

Then, just as he perceived that the trees ahead of him were thinning fast and that he was about to emerge from the swamplands, he received another shock, for Jill Pedlar — much less the young lady now in her blue shirt, well-scrubbed Levis and cuffed back Stetson — stepped into his path from behind a clump of bushes and threw up her hands, bringing him to a halt. 'I heard the shooting over yonder,' she said. 'I saw you riding towards the sea an hour or so back, and then I saw Jack Starbuck and his boys heading in the same direction. I — I figured you might be in trouble and — and came this way to see.'

A remarkable piece of anticipation, he thought, but he'd no part of his mind to give to it just then. 'I need a horse,' he gasped. 'Can you get me one?'

'Where's yours, Sheriff?'

'Long story,' he said shortly. 'Can you?'

'I can try,' she said. 'But you'll have to let me hide you up while I go about it.'

Nodding reluctantly, he supposed that would have to do for the moment.

# 6

Giving her chin a jerk, the girl faced away from Kane. She began to hurry eastwards, walking and jogging by turns, and he imitated her movements as they went along. Presently she turned towards a tall tree that stood on her right and went to the back of it. Still following her closely, Kane saw a rope ladder hanging down from the branches above and, looking up, made out a tree-house which had been built on the foundations provided by the bole's main fork and the branches that radiated about the joint. 'Up there,' Jill Pedlar said; and, taking hold of the rope ladder with her hands, she placed a foot on the first of the plaited rungs and began to climb, screwing and twisting her way aloft with a skill that had clearly been developed by many similar climbs in the past.

Kane followed her upwards, though with much less agility and at half the speed, but he completed the ascent without any real difficulty and entered the tree-house while the girl held open the canvas flap which covered the entrance. After that she let the strip of waterproof material fall back into place once more and withdrew from the entrance, passing round the back of her visitor and halting square with the window-space in the western side of the tree-house. Then she pointed to the view provided by the height of the great sycamore in which they were perched.

Gazing over the blonde's head, the sheriff found himself looking out across a semi-arc of treetops towards a panoramic view of the triple-armed Pedlar's Claw itself, with its lagoons, green-topped morasses, and islands of reeds. It was at once obvious to him that a watcher from up here had a rather broken but adequate view of the woodland floor right out to the swamps, and he could not dismiss the feeling that Jill Pedlar must have been up here for some while earlier and watched him heading into the orbit of the tree-house before descending to meet him. It could be that she had come here from her home immediately after spotting Jack Starbuck and his outlaws entering the swamp. Now why would she have done that — unless she had feared that the doings foreshadowed by the presence of so many men in Pedlar's Claw would eventually spread to include her? An action of the kind would have to suggest that she did indeed have something to hide and that her property could later be searched — as might be happening right now. Kane would have liked to question her about it then; but he felt that his own interests must come first and that it was vital to save time, so he merely said: 'I didn't know you had this tree-house, Jill.'

'You weren't meant to,' she answered. 'It's been my secret retreat for years. Dad built it for me when I was a child.

He couldn't look after me properly after mother died, and he felt that this place kept me safe while he was over in the swamps killing 'gators.'

'A kid's delight,' Kane acknowledged. 'So you're going to run home and get me a horse, hey?'

'Yes, I'll do my best to bring my own riding horse back for you,' she said uneasily.

He breathed deeply, quelling his impatience; for he perceived that, despite his own need to get her moving without delay, he would have to make it plain to her that he knew what was going on out here — and how it almost certainly involved her — so he told her, in a hundred or so well-chosen and rapidly delivered words, all that had recently happened to him in Pedlar's Claw and what he had learned from the story that had been pieced together there by Jack Starbuck, Colonel Barris and Amos Sweetman, concluding: 'It's my notion your father moved that treasure from its hiding place in the swamps to one at your home, girl. Lookit, Jilly! I've no intention of making trouble for you, if it can be avoided — because I want to believe that you're basically innocent of any crime — but it may be that you've got anxious for your future, and I want to advise you not to try hanging on to something that isn't yours.' He gazed steadily into the big blue eyes that she had turned to him. 'It's sort of a word to the wise, Jill. You help me all you can, in whatever circumstances may come up — hiding no damned thing whatsoever — and I'll do everything in my power to see that you come to no harm through the actions of your pa or anybody else. Got me?'

'I'm not — not really sure what — what you're talking about,' the girl faltered. 'This is the first that I've heard about any — '

'Cut it out, Jill!' Kane cautioned impatiently. 'You remember what I've said. Now go and fetch that horse for me. You don't have to be afraid of those outlaws. I'll soon settle their hash once I've got the help I need from Rockford.'

'Didn't you say that Jack Starbuck and those villains of his have it in mind to take my home apart?' the blonde asked. 'Supposing I find them at it when I — '

'Homes can be put together again,' the sheriff interrupted grimly. 'That's all you need remember this afternoon. Now — get going!'

She hesitated, chalk-white and shaking — not at all the confident young woman with whom Kane had talked in town that morning — and he seemed to detect some hope dying within her. It could be that, instinctively, she was trying to create some weakness in him, so he held himself rigid and implacable — downright threatening in fact — because he felt that he must impress upon her as deeply as possible that her only safety lay in absolute obedience to his will. If she failed him, she must understand that she

115

would fail herself in like degree. Iron bars did a prison make, and hemp a rope that hanged. Now visibly shrinking from him, she slipped past him to the door and backed out on to the rope ladder from beneath the canvas which covered the exit. In a moment more she had passed from view, and he could feel the vibration in the tree-house created by her descent to the ground.

Kane let go a pent up breath. He allowed himself to relax a little and look around the interior of the tree-house. He saw standing, on the floorboards at the back of the box-like structure, a small table and a chair of similar dimensions. On the table lay a book or two, some fancy sewing and a set of tea things — proof enough that Jill Pedlar still used her childhood retreat almost as much as she had while growing up. Everything in sight was well-kept and spotless — for all the spores of decay that the nearby swamp kept sending into the wood's environs — and the cool freshness of the girl

116

herself seemed to have invested the tree-house with a sense of her purity. He did start feeling a kind of pity for Jill Pedlar in the emptiness of her life — and glimpsed how easy it would be to forgive any thoughts of wrong that might be circling the fringes of her mind — but there could be no circumstances to excuse crime and he must not go soft or let his own purpose waiver. A game was being played out here, and he must stick completely to the rules. He had warned the girl of what to expect, and the rest was for her to decide. There could be no other way — up to and including the death, if it should so turn out.

The minutes dragged by, and the tension within Kane screwed tighter and tighter. He sought to relieve it, muttering under his breath, but he couldn't pace because the room about him was too restrictive, and he couldn't sit down because Jill Pedlar's chair was plainly too frail to support his weight; so he went to the window-space and looked out at the ever-changing patterns of sunlight and shadow upon the swamplands towards the sea, drumming his fingers on the framework before him while he did so; and he was becoming quite worried about Jill Pedlar's safety — since he had been well aware that he was sending her into real danger when he had asked her to fetch him a horse — when he heard movements below him that sent him to the other side of the tree-house and a spy-hole in the wall there which revealed the presence of the blonde and a reddish-brown mare on the ground below his enclosed perch. 'Adam!' the girl called up to him.

But he was already on the move and, backing out through the exit, picked up the rope ladder with his feet and descended from the tree-house at the best pace he could manage, joining the blonde soon enough on the piece of open ground where she stood with the mount. 'Thanks, Jill,' he said. 'Was there anybody at your house?'

'They were all there,' she answered, 'but so engrossed in turning the place upside down — as you said they had in mind — that it wasn't difficult for me to fetch my horse out of its stable and creep away.'

'Good girl,' he responded, wondering what level of craft and how many anxious moments his trite words of praise were trying to recompense. 'Did you spot any riders on the land nearby?'

'No.'

'Well, that's helpful,' Kane said, though there was a doubtful note in his voice. 'But I'd better behave as if they're there anyhow.' He nodded briefly to himself. 'You'd better get back up top. Stay in the tree-house until I come shouting for you — however long that takes.'

'All right,' she replied. 'Take care.'

'I aim to,' he assured her, preparing to mount up; but that was as far as he got, for three men — Tony Essen and two others from the Starbuck gang — burst out of some undergrowth nearby and covered them with revolvers.

'Get your paws up!' Essen ordered through his split and swollen lips. 'Figured you and Adam Kane had got us truly hornswoggled, eh, Jilly? Sorry, sweetheart! Your old dad told me about that tree-house of yours long ago. He said it was your habit to run off there when things were gettin' you down. Not too sharp today, eh?'

'Botheration!' the girl exploded.

'That's right, honey,' Essen taunted — 'have yourself a swear. It don't half relieve the mind!'

'Now what?' the blonde asked dismally, just missing Kane's eye and her face aged many a year by the clenching of her jaw and the sighing flare of her nostrils.

'Don't you fret none, my love,' Essen soothed, though still mocking. 'I'll look after you. You don't have to worry about Jack Starbuck and the rest. I can take care o' them.'

'All evidence being to the contrary,'

the sheriff couldn't help remarking.

'You shut your mouth, Kane,' Essen ordered viciously, 'or I'll put a bullet in it.'

'Was I Jack Starbuck,' the lawman said bitterly, 'and had a man of your loyalty riding with me, I'd feed you the whole gun — and not necessarily through the mouth!'

'Just listen to him,' said the older of Essen's two companions, a fat, round-faced man, with small features, almost hairless brows, and a sagging belly. 'You ain't going to put up with that, are you, Tony?'

'Aw, he's blamed ignorant!' Essen declared. 'Ignorant lot out of Rockford. The army used 'em to dig latrines and graves most days.'

'You've got a point there, Tony,' Kane acknowledged. 'I noticed how much time you spent with a shovel in your hands.'

The fat man spluttered into mirth, and the third outlaw, a spindle-limbed, dog-faced character, with jutting teeth and a hairy nose covered with blackheads, allowed himself a mean little chuckle too.

'Barney Soames,' Essen said darkly, slanting a glance at the fat man and gritting audibly, 'you can dry up as fast as you like. Same goes for you, Bonzo Ryder. You hear?'

'If you can't take it, Tony,' Bonzo Ryder yapped in reply, 'don't hand it out. Son, I suggest you tell that yeller-haired gal to take hold of that hoss again. I wanna get back to the Pedlar house. Knowin' the rest of our boys, if they turn up them jewels in our absence, they're liable to head for the Big Muddy — or somewhere far off — with our share as well as their own. True?'

'Jill,' Essen snapped, indicating that the girl should do what Ryder had suggested; then, closing on Kane — who had already stepped back from the horse, threw a sudden left hook at the sheriff's jaw.

Kane had been half expecting

something of the sort, and swayed away from the punch, but nevertheless started his movement a split second too late and still received pretty well the entire force of the punch on the side of his jaw. The blow knocked him flat on his back and he lay there with his brain spinning again.

'That's more like it,' Ryder approved.

'Tony, I didn't know you had it in you!' Soames announced, stomach wobbling with a new merriment. 'But don't try it on Jack Starbuck.'

'Or me again,' Kane advised, eyes narrowing into fiery slits as he shoved himself to his feet and dusted off his backside.

'Or you'll what?' Essen inquired disdainfully. 'Get moving. You know the way. You, too, Jill!'

Kane took the first stride. They followed the lightly marked path by which the great sycamore which supported the tree-house was most easily approached. It took them a short distance eastwards, then turned to the left and bore them out of the remaining trees and undergrowth on to the northern grass. After that — still only the faintest of traces upon the ground — it bent left again and led them westwards in the direction of the white walls and fences of the Pedlar property about half a mile away. Over there the sheriff saw at once a number of loose horses cropping outside the garden gate. He also made out Colonel Barris and Captain Starbuck. They were standing outside the front door of the cottage and gazing intently towards the spot where the two prisoners and their outlaw escort must now be visible to them.

The party closed on the cottage at a steady pace, but even so it took a few minutes to cover the ground. Thus Kane was given time to take in detail, and he noted, as they neared the property, that his mount was among those feeding outside the Pedlar home, which meant that Starbuck and company must have seen a possible profit in the beast and brought it out of the swamp with them. Kane was pleased about that, for the mount's close proximity prompted glimmerings of hope in his brain, but he realized that these vague notions of escape were unlikely to burgeon in the near future, since Tony Essen and friends were obviously keeping the tightest of watches on Jill and himself, if only to impress the two ex-army officers who went on watching them as fixedly as ever from the Pedlar doorstep. 'Any trouble?' Jack Starbuck eventually called.

'None, Jack!' Essen responded, as the prisoners and their escort reached the garden gate. 'Everything went like clockwork!'

'Best for you it did, Tony!' Starbuck informed him, both his harsh tones and the sternness of his expression warning Essen that any attempts to ingratiate himself anew with his astute and hard-fisted boss would get him nowhere. 'Get those two in here, boy, and look sharp about it!'

Kane and the blonde were hurried up the garden path. Hands shoved them and gun muzzles prodded. They were taken into the house, then through to the parlour, whence Barris and Starbuck had retreated a little ahead of them and taken up new stands, one on either side of the fireplace. The room was in a terrible state, and the girl gave a sob at the sight of it. The mats had been thrown this way and that, cupboard doors stood open, drawers hung out with their contents spilling from them, the dining table lay upon its side, and a timepiece and a variety of ornaments had been smashed all over the flagstones of the floor. It was indeed a shameful mess — a product of the most wickedly gleeful vandalism — but neither the colonel nor the captain showed the least sympathy for Jill Pedlar, and Starbuck seized her by the upper arms and shook her with an unrestrained violence before throwing her backwards into an armchair and saying: 'You've hidden that treasure up well, missy! We've found nothing so far. But we're going to have that loot before we've done — and you are going to tell us where it is. Right now!'

'I'm not!' Jill flung back defiantly. 'I can't! I don't know where your wretched treasure is, Captain Starbuck. My father said nothing to me about it. He was suffering too badly to think about much else.'

'You're a liar!' Starbuck returned harshly. 'If you tell me the truth, girl, you'll take no further harm. I don't like hurting women; it goes right against the grain. But if you keep telling me lies, missy, you're going to get hurt. Now do yourself a favour and tell me where you've got those jewels hidden. Do that, and we'll be out of here faster than two shakes of a dog's tail. Colonel?'

'He speaks truly, Miss Pedlar,' Alonzo Barris assured her.

'But I can't tell you what I don't know,' the blonde pleaded.

127

'I say you do know!' Starbuck insisted. 'Tony Essen told me that your father told him he was worried as to what would happen to you when he was gone. He must have spoken to you along the same lines. It stands to reason, g'dammit! You know where your nestegg is all right. We want it, but that's all we want. Once we've got it, we'll go. Honour bright!'

'What do you know about honour?' the girl inquired scathingly, while cowering away from the captain's towering presence. 'You're a disgrace to the uniform you once wore!'

Starbuck released a long and heavy sigh. 'It seems you insist on being hurt, missy. Very well.'

'Punch me then!' Jill Pedlar cried. 'Kick me, slap me around! Do what you want, you big brute! But I can't tell you what I don't know! Not possibly!'

'Oh, I'm not going to draw blood,' Starbuck said mildly, though the leer which had replaced the expression of animal violence on his features was even more frightening than any look that had gone before. 'I had a lot to do with the Chinese at one time. They are the world's greatest masters at inflicting tortures that create maximum pain yet leave very little evidence on the body that they were ever carried out. The worst one is scraping the bones with a steel needle. But that one would be too terrible to inflict on a lovely little thing like you. I doubt you'd stay conscious under it long enough anyhow. No, I'm going to use a torture on you that will leave no mark behind it at all. It's known as torment by water. Just drip, drip, drip — drip; right in the centre of the forehead. You may resist for a while, girl, but there'll be pain enough to drive you mad in the end!'

'You fiend!' the blonde choked in response.

'So I am,' Jack Starbuck acknowledged regretfully. 'But I'm mostly a good fiend. All I want to be is a rich one — and then I shan't have to be a fiend at all. Not to you anyway. Some other girl maybe? One who'll take pay for it?' Chuckling to himself, he reached down and knocked the girl's hat off, then stroked her hair and let his fingers stray gently down her face and neck, adding after a moment or two: 'How a crabby old tree like Ivan Pedlar produced so choice a fruit, I'll never know. One o' the mysteries of the age.'

'Do stop toying with her, Captain,' Colonel Barris said, sounding distinctly irritated. 'You're starting to act as if our time were our own. We don't know that it is. You and your men ride the country as if you own it. The girl has to talk. Make her.' He paused significantly. 'Perhaps I'm leaving too much to you.'

'No,' Starbuck said warningly, 'just the right amount. You needn't get anxious, Colonel. She'll talk soon enough.'

Barris nodded curtly, clearly wishing to say more, but just as plainly not feeling that to be politic.

Kane, watching closely, saw Starbuck

smile secretly to himself, then retreated as far into the background as possible when he saw that Starbuck was considering what to do about him; but the captain's mouth twitched dismissively as he appeared to opt for one thing at a time; and, plucking Jill Pedlar out of the chair in which she was still cringeing, he marched her into a room adjoining the present one — the kitchen, Kane believed — and shouted peremptorily for Tony Essen to attend him 'pronto'. Essen came blundering indoors from the garden — still possessed of an abnormal willingness to please — and he went diving in pursuit of the gang-boss. Then Kane heard the order given for Tony to produce a bucket from somewhere and put a hole in its bottom — cover the hole with a piece of fine cloth, fill the bucket with water next, then hang the contraption from a beam and make sure that it produced a steady dripping which would strike the floor, droplet by droplet, at exactly the same spot all the time. Tony Essen declared that he could visualise exactly what the captain wanted, and after that there was a great to-ing and fro-ing next door as he went to work.

Presently Kane heard the banging of a hammer, and the ringing of steel as a punch was dropped. Then, as further sounds of industry became audible, Starbuck began hectoring again and finding fault with everything Tony Essen did; but, for all his instructions and promptings with the boot, nothing happened quickly, and well over an hour went by before the sheriff heard sounds of water being poured from one container into another and other noises followed that suggested a heavy bucket was being supported by one man while the other tied it to a beam in the ceiling. 'Yes, it'll do, Tony!' Starbuck eventually declared. 'Now lookee here. I've got that girl trussed up, as you can see. So bring her over here and stretch her out upon the floor — forehead right under that drip.'

There was a long pause, filled with a crying from Jill Pedlar and a grunting from Tony Essen as he manhandled her body across the adjoining room and presumably into the position which Stabuck had commanded, for the only words from the captain now were those which expressed satisfaction with what his underling had done. 'Right you are!' he finally announced. 'Let's see how long you can stand that, my girl!'

Jill Palmer mouthed some new defiance at him, but the listening Kane received an impression from the name-calling and such that the girl was losing heart and he didn't know whether to be glad or sad about that — for he didn't want the blonde to suffer pain at the hands of their captors — whether she was actually holding out on them or simply a victim of the situation — but his sympathies in that direction were soon stifled, for he next heard Starbuck say, and in the most gloating of tones: 'I'm going to leave you for a while, missy, to consider the folly of your ways. It's time I arranged for that sheriff acquaintance of ours to be taken care of. See you later, eh?'

Bracing himself, Kane waited for the captain to re-enter the parlour. He reckoned it was back to the swamp for him.

# 7

Starbuck stalked back into the parlour a moment later. He was closely followed by a dishevelled and tired-looking Tony Essen. The pair exchanged glances with Colonel Barris — who was still standing by and showing signs of boredom — and then they gazed directly at Kane, the captain with a jaw-thrusting, flint-eyed belligerence and Essen with the spiteful glee of an unpleasant child who was about to see one of his dearest wishes consummated. 'Soames — Ryder!' Captain Starbuck bellowed. 'Show yourselves, you lazy, good-for-nothing sons-of-bitches! Get yourselves in here this instant!'

Running steps became audible outside the door to Kane's left which communicated with the garden, and the round-faced Soames lurched into the parlour a moment or two later, pursed lips puffing an admission of his excessive belly-weight, while the dog-faced Ryder craned into view a split-second after that, not quite with his tongue lolling, but displaying much of the shrinking self-abasement on the canine breed nevertheless. 'What is it, Jack?' Soames wheezed.

'Job for you, my man,' Starbuck responded. 'That lawman has lived too long. See him off!'

'Here?'

'Take him back to the swamp, you damned fool!' the captain cried. 'Do it there.'

'There's a storm coming up, Cap'n,' Bonzo Ryder said over the point of his fat comrade's left shoulder. And, as if to back up the outlaw's statement, thunder rumbled off to the southwest of the house, a grumbling presence that intensified perceptibly as all present listened to it. 'The light's goin' too. You'll excuse me, suh, but that swamp ain't no place to be in bad light and pourin' rain. These tempests that blow up off the Gulf are like the very wrath o' God!'

'What would you know about that, mister?' Colonel Barris asked in faintly amused contempt. 'But he's right, you know, Starbuck. Pedlar's Claw is no place to send those fellows in a thunder-storm.'

'So blow out his brains and throw him down the well!' Starbuck snarled. 'What the hell do I care, so long as he's dead and done for.'

'Captain,' Barris said with courtesy and obvious care, 'much as I'd prefer it otherwise, it appears to me — what with this change of weather and the lengthening day — that we're going to be stuck in this cottage overnight. We'll need water for our own uses. A dead man adds no flavour to the liquor. Put Sheriff Kane down the well at dawn tomorrow, by all means, but — '

'It seems I get an argument every time I open my mouth,' Starbuck interrupted grumpily — his expression confessing, though, that he was too wise a man to ignore the valid ones. 'All right, Tony. You and your two pals can bundle Kane into the kitchen and tie him up. He'll keep till the morning, fresh as a daisy. Then down the well he goes — and damn the water!'

The three badmen closed upon Kane. They pushed and shoved him into the kitchen, where they tripped him to the floor and Essen put a foot on his face to hold him flat. Then Bonzo Ryder withdrew for a few moments and reappeared holding a rope. After that the trio went to work on the lawman with a variety of loops and knots, securing him from the shoulders down and leaving him quite helpless, for his wrists were bound over his tailbone and his ankles had been drawn up towards his spine to complete the hog-tie. Finally, the evil trio let fly at him with the toes of their boots, each giving him a few kicks that bruised his belly and ribs. This punishment left him winded and feeling horribly sick, but the three men stopped it before they did any real harm and walked back into the parlour, where the injured sheriff heard them laughing with Starbuck over what they appeared to regard as their cleverness.

Slowly recovering his breath, Kane shut his eyes and summoned up the healing powers of his mind to reduce the stitch in his lower abdomen and soothe away that pain which filled the middle of his body generally. This process needed time to take effect and, while he was concentrating upon it, he heard the storm of which Bonzo Ryder had spoken roll up overhead. There it cracked and boomed with an ear-splitting violence, and the dagger-swift brilliance of its lightning penetrated the sheriff's eyelashes with such vividness that it burned images on Kane's retinas which remained present for minutes after the main fury of the storm had passed. Opening his eyes again, he lay there softly groaning, while the shadow of the storm moved on and left behind it only the slant of its pursuing rain and the bluster of the wind which accompanied it.

Soon the atmosphere began to clear, and Kane's suffering became more bearable. Wondering exactly where Jill Pedlar was located and how she was getting on, Kane gazed around the kitchen — which was about as plain as a room of its kind could get, with a stone sink under the window, a cooking range that was heated by the fireplace, and a battered cupboard and some shelves — and saw that the table had been shoved aside to clear the flagstoned floor at the centre of the place to make space for Jill Pedlar to lie full-length under a beam of mahogany from which hung a bucket which was releasing steady drips of water onto the girl's forehead. She had been bound in a star fashion and anchored to points around the kitchen which held her rigidly in position. She had not been hurt in any obvious manner, but was moaning to herself, and Kane imagined that she must have

140

been feeling the cumulative effects of the subtle Chinese torture long before this and would soon begin suffering in earnest. He spoke her name, but she didn't answer, and he decided to let it go at that. He couldn't help her, and she couldn't help him. Yes, he'd heard of moral support, but it was one of those things that was fine when pain wasn't around. He had found it quite useless when physical agony was making hay of human resistance. If a body hurt, then it hurt, and there wasn't a whole lot of room for much else.

Kane was stuck with his thoughts. The day had been a bad one for him. It wasn't so much that he'd made a mess of his work as that everything had gone wrong just when he had seemed to be getting it right. It had been rare poor luck where his meeting with Jill Pedlar at the edge of the nearby trees had been concerned. He might have known that Tony Essen would have heard something about the girl's retreat while visiting her father, and he should have realized that the fact that she had been missing from her home when the outlaws had arrived there from the swamp — and not forgetting the possibilities that had been inherent in his escape from Jack Starbuck and company — would have prompted the chance that she would be sought at her tree-house and thus give away his presence too. The only good thing in that episode had been the sudden coming of the storm from the Gulf of Mexico and the reprieve that it had earned him. If he could only escape from his bonds, there might still be hope for him in his own ingenuity; but he was all too sure that no effort on his part could bring him freedom. Wrestling with a tightly knotted rope could be a noisy business, and there were too many ears around the cottage that would be likely to pick up the sounds of his struggle. It would be crazy to risk it. If he were caught trying to escape, he didn't doubt that retribution would be instant and incapacitating — if not actually fatal.

The sheriff drifted into a kind of reverie. He let time go by. This did little to assist his plight, but did take the raw edge off his fears, and he was calm within himself — if a little disturbed by the incessant dripping of the water nearby and the feelings of empathy which were evoked when he heard the occasional soft groaning from his fellow prisoner lying in what was now the late evening light — when Jack Starbuck entered the kitchen again, a glowing oil lamp held in his right hand and shadow streaming in almost ghostly distortions across the walls and ceiling. Ignoring Kane's presence completely, the captain asked conversationally of the girl: 'How goes it, Jill?'

'Go and fry!' the blonde wrenched out.

'You are a singularly brave little idiot, aren't you?' Starbuck observed, chuckling a mixture of admiration and surprise. 'Why keep it up? This is going to be your one and only chance to free yourself from that torment for a long time. I aim to snatch a few hours' sleep. When I get off, it takes the Crack of Doom to wake me. Again I urge you to be sensible. Tell me where you've hidden those jewels and I'll free you immediately. You'll be able to climb into your own little bed and spend the night in peaceful slumber. If you don't — Well, you know what you've already endured. You'll have to suffer a great deal more of the same. I aim to break you, missy! Remember, that loot has no value for you. You'll never be able to sell it off. What good's a fortune that's worth less to you than a shot bunny? You're not a fool, Jill — you're just behaving like one.'

'Go and fry!' the girl repeated.

'I'm not impressed, Starbuck,' said Colonel Barris's voice from the entrance to the next room. 'Your Chinese torture doesn't seem to work.'

'Oh, it will,' the captain promised — 'it will.'

'It ought to have done so before now,' Barris said firmly.

'It will,' Starbuck insisted waspishly — 'it will!'

'Miss Pedlar?' Barris queried.

No sound issued from the girl. But the water kept on dripping down.

'Let her rot,' Starbuck said shortly. 'She'll give in finally, Colonel — she must!'

'If she hasn't by first light, mister,' Barris said, 'I shall strongly advise you to let Amos Sweetman take over the matter of torturing her from you. I promise you that Sweetman will get the result you need within minutes. I have seen him get to work with red hot iron.'

'Yes, you damned Yankee butcher!' Starbuck seethed; and the listening Adam Kane almost sympathised with the man.

'Captain, captain,' the colonel breathed, sounding a hint more than pained. 'As one officer to another?'

'To hell with that!'

145

'Nevertheless, Captain Starbuck, I shall advise.'

'So long as you don't insist!' Starbuck fired back, facing round and making his return to the parlour, lamp still held high and his shadow again striking across the walls and ceiling like a phantom presence. 'Let's stop this wrangling and get some sleep.'

The light passed into the next room, and the door squeaked on its hinges as it was pulled to within an inch or so of shut. Further movements were audible around the interior of the cottage for a few minutes longer, then all became still, and Kane got the impression that Starbuck and company were all asleep in whatever corners they had found for themselves, though he didn't doubt that a guard had been set outside, for these men were breaking the law close to civilised parts and could not afford to be taken by surprise in any circumstances at all.

Kane tried to slip back into his reverie, but the recent happenings seemed to have driven out his earlier calm for good. It was night outside the kitchen window now, and a full moon kept throwing its disturbing glow through the panes and then snuffing out, proof of considerable cloud-banks flying above the house in a fairly broken state. The sheriff felt a clammy dampness creeping over his skin, and this suggested that there could be further rain to come. His discomfort made him think hard about the far greater misery of Jill Pedlar's ordeal, and he realized that he had been growing puzzled by her remarkable tolerance of pain. He didn't know a lot about the Chinese and their tortures, but he had heard that no race had ever bettered them in that line, and the water torment was rated as among the most effective means of making a prisoner talk ever devised. Jill had survived hours of suffering and was still doing so in relative silence. She had not once screamed out in real pain, or shouted in madness. That was indeed worth questioning, for, so far as Kane was aware, she was around average in most repects and had never shown a greater ability to withstand pain than anybody else.

The sheriff suspected that Colonel Barris had been thinking along similar lines just now. Within the scope of what observations he could make, Barris had been justified in doubting Starbuck's torture measures. Now a peculiar suspicion began to permeate Kane's mind. Had the gang-boss left a virtually imperceptible play in the bonds that held the girl apparently rigid which allowed her to move her head to the tiny extent necessary to prevent the water dripping out of the pierced bucket above her from falling exactly on the centre of her forehead every time? The torture's lack of success so far certainly suggested something of the sort.

Could Starbuck have spoiled his crude lay-out by accident? No; Kane couldn't believe that. If he had done something of the kind, he would have realized his mistake before now and put it right. Which would have to mean that the error on his part had been deliberate. Planned, perhaps, ahead of the event. Possibly when Jill had returned to the cottage to sneak out her horse for the escaping Kane.

Were Starbuck and Jill Pedlar in cahoots? Did they plan to attempt decamping with the Aztec treasure and keeping it for themselves? The pattern was there, and Kane could see the linkage. Starbuck had spoken of keeping an eye on Tony Essen, and that would have brought him into these parts. If Jill and he had met — with Tony as the unconscious link between them — many things could have become possible. Jill, man-starved, would not have found it hard to fall in love with the handsome and devil-may-care captain. And Starbuck was a natural ladies' man who would always be on the look-out for a new bustle. Yes, it was entirely possible that a spur-of-the-moment arrangement had been worked out between the pair. Yet how was it going to operate? The whole thing would have to be chancy and depend on very good timing. But it nevertheless remained true that if you had the courage to dare, you could often win through while others hesitated. Had he entered another dimension of this remarkable crime? It certainly felt like it. After all, he had been feeling an instinctive mistrust of Jill Pedlar throughout the day — without, in his wish to disregard his suspicions, even glimpsing until now how far into the wrong-doing she could actually be.

Kane halted his speculations there. He couldn't let his mind run on too far. Now he started going over the bits and pieces which his brain had lately assembled and began putting them into new relationships, hoping that he would get an even clearer picture of what could be going on, but the original one remained the best and most reasonable. He was sure that Jack Starbuck and Jill Pedlar had a set-up here that was designed to bamboozle both Colonel Barris and the members of the captain's gang. Essentially the pair were, as he had already perceived, trying to create an opportunity to flee the cottage tonight, unbeknownst to the rest of the crooks, and escape up country before the others could grasp exactly what had occurred and give chase. And that appeared to be the sum total of it up to the moment. Jill and Starbuck simply wanted to deceive their fellow conspirators for as long as possible. Kane didn't doubt that the blonde had the Aztec treasure stashed somewhere real handy, if totally unexpected, and that the need to pick it up would delay her and the captain by a minute only.

Some doubt had to remain, of course, and the sheriff fretted among his uncertainties for quite a while longer until, as he judged, around midnight the door connecting the prison room with the parlour creaked softly again and somebody entered the kitchen, pausing for just an instant before starting to creep forward once more. Tensing up, Kane drew a deep breath and held it, releasing the air only at the slowest of rates. There was no light in the kitchen to see by — for the entrant was carrying no lamp and the moon outside was in another of its dark spells — but the sheriff had already sensed that the man nearby was Jack Starbuck and that the captain was moving towards him.

No word was spoken, and hardly a sound was made. Then the unseen man bent at Kane's side — his breath playing softly on the lawman's face — and began to pluck at the knots which secured the captive with strong fingers, loosening them by a considerable amount without actually undoing them; and, as he felt the pressure of the bindings on his limbs relax to the extent that he could actually move them again, Kane believed that he was to be freed entirely; but then the easement of the rope about him ceased and he was left still sufficiently tied to make seeking instant freedom impossible — yet with the inner awareness that he could free himself now without too many writhings or much of a struggle.

What the dickens was Starbuck up to here?

# 8

The hands which had partially untied Kane withdrew from the bonds that still held him more or less fast, and their owner retreated across the kitchen floor to where Jill Pedlar lay invisible to her fellow prisoner in the darkness. A number of barely audible actions now reached Kane's ears, and he received the impression that a very sharp knife was being used to cut the blonde free from her rather complex bindings as swiftly as could be managed. He seemed to hear sliced sections of the rope falling away from the girl's limbs, and made out something of the suffering thus induced as she groaned softly to herself.

Muttered words were exchanged between Starbuck and the blonde. The captain's were rather impatient ones, and Kane sensed the intense need for haste beyond him, but he also judged that Jill Pedlar was being forced erect and compelled to use her legs before the cramping lack of circulation in her limbs had even started to ease. He feared that the pair would fall over something in the darkness and arouse the entire house. Pray God a disaster of that kind would not occur! Just now he didn't care what Jill and the captain did, or where they went. He was almost free, and the only desire he seemed to have left in him was to be completely so once more.

Then the moon burst into view again. Its light gleamed outside the window, and shafts of white radiance entered the kitchen and pushed back its gloom. The glow revealed Jill Pedlar standing erect — though half crippled — and Kane saw the captain lift her with one arm towards the further end of the room's northern wall, where he reached for the latch on a door which had not been opened up to now. The latch lifted and the door opened at Starbuck's pull. A smell of the sea and the wet land about the dwelling entered with the sudden chill of the breeze.

Ignoring the stiffened girl's persisting incapacity, the captain swung her out soundlessly into the night and they hovered there for a moment like shadows. Then Starbuck drew the door shut in their wake and let the latch settle back into place under the checking pressure of his thumb. The girl and he were instantly part of the world without, and the faint gusting of the wind covered any rumour of their departure. They were gone, as if they had never been — and Kane's spine crept in response to the idea — though the bucket hanging from the beam yonder still dripped as monotonously as ever.

Getting full control of himself, Kane held his breath and listened at the silence which once more enclosed him. Everybody in the cottage still seemed to be deeply asleep. He must take his chance immediately. Willing himself to it — since he had his own cramp pains and inertia to overcome — he began easing his arms out of the bonds that now slackly encompassed them and, after a minute or two of the most careful writhings, freed them totally. After that he forced the turns of rope down his body, releasing the hog-tie in the process, and then unfastened the knots at his ankles. Finally he pushed the bonds off his feet and kicked them aside. He was free — and it brought him a wonderful feeling of relief.

His efforts, far from huge, had left him drained all the same, and he lay where he was for a short while, allowing his energies to recoup and the singing of blood in his brain to subside, for he realized that to stand up suddenly and go reeling across the floor into a heavy fall would instantly lose him whatever advantage he had been granted here. When he did rise, he made no attempt to stride out in the direction of the back door but held his ground and asked himself as sensibly as he could what his next move was to be.

Then, as he began to see what had been foisted on him here, an amused smile came to his lips. Starbuck might be all kinds of a villain, but he was also smart as paint. For he, too, wherever he was at this moment, was relying on how the sheriff would act next, since he had obviously gambled that, if he made it possible for Kane to free himself shortly after he, Starbuck, and the girl had fled, the lawman would feel obliged, for his own safety's sake, to use the more immediate half of the opportunity with which he had been presented to arrest Colonel Barris and the members of the Starbuck gang before attempting anything further afield — thus protecting the captain's getaway with Jill Pedlar and the Aztec jewels.

It was indeed clever — and the wiser course would undoubtedly be to promptly arrest the colonel and the crooks that Starbuck had deserted, if only to remove the larger force against him from the future doings — but the sheer audacity of the captain's action had aroused Kane's own contrariness. He'd be damned if he would give Starbuck the later satisfaction of knowing that his craft had been beyond the lawman's power to circumvent. He wasn't going to let his enemy have the last laugh here. Not that he could take any clever counter measures himself, but he could risk the dangers of letting Barris stay free and do the exact opposite of what the captain was so subtly impelling him to do now. When all was said and done, it was the treasure which lay at the heart of this business, and the best way of thwarting Starbuck completely would be to come up from behind and take it from him. Yes, that was the only answer that covered all. He would ride in pursuit of the captain and Jill Pedlar as soon as he possibly could.

Kane began to walk slowly and stiffly towards the back door. He reached the exit without making a sound.

Opening up, he stepped outside and shut the door behind him again no less silently. Breathing in the freshness of the wind, he saw his shadow lying in the moonlight to his right and gazed in that direction. A piece of garden stretched on that hand. He moved into it, bent on reaching the ground where he had last seen his own and the outlaws' horses standing — since he was all too aware that he could not do a thing until he had a mount under him — and he came to the picket fence at the edge of the property and stepped over it, determined to stay in motion and ignore the risks that could be lying about him.

Still heading to the right, he slanted off in the direction of the ground on which he hoped the horses would be and saw them still there. They were black shapes that barely stirred on the moon-whitened graze opposite the front gate of the house. The creatures ignored his approach, and he walked into their midst and narrowed his gaze a trifle as he sought the familiar outlines of his own beast. He thought he saw his mount at the further side of the bunch — and was relieved at how easy all this seemed to be — when a sentry suddenly rose out of a sitting position on the left of the nearby gate, where he had probably been dozing up to then and, thrusting out a rifle, said sharply: 'Who is that? Is that you, Jesse Weems? What're you doing out here?'

'Yeah, it's me,' Kane agreed without hesitation, adding what gruffness he could generate to disguise his voice into the kind of sound that might come from any man of his size. 'Just seeing to my horse.'

'Blame critter don't need seein' to at this time o' the night,' the man behind the rifle said querulously. 'You're supposed to be indoors and fast asleep.'

'Fast asleep like you were?' the sheriff jested, sauntering towards the other with his hands thrust deep in his trouser-pockets.

'I wasn't asleep!'

'You were too,' Kane contradicted, closing on his man in the same lazy manner and trying to ignore the increasingly intent stare that the outlaw had fixed on him. 'I came out of the front door, pal, walked through the gate beside you, and over to the horses. You didn't see or hear a blamed thing.' He chuckled. 'You were sure sending 'em home, boy!'

'What is this?' the guard yelped. 'You ain't Jesse Weems! You're that doggone sheriff — !'

Kane snatched his fists out of his pockets and hit the other just then. The blows were a left hook followed by a right. The sheriff had been winding himself up to deliver them, and both landed exactly on target, smashing the sentry's mouth shut. Down went the man, and he lay absolutely still. In fact Kane couldn't see him rising again for several minutes and, after helping himself to the other's pistol and holstering it, he faced about and went back to seeking his horse, finding the animal at the spot where he thought he had glimpsed it a short while before.

Gripping his mount at the bit, Kane led it clear of the other animals in the vicinity. After that he walked it in the direction of the picket fence and used the palings to guide him back to the northern side of the cottage adjacent, for it was obvious now that he couldn't just spring into leather and gallop out at hazard. He must get a reliable idea of his quarry's line of flight, and only finding actual sign could help him in that. Tracking at night was normally only for the gifted few; but, with the moon as bright as it was right now and the ground as thoroughly sodden, he ought to be able to discover sign somewhere nearby and come up with the pointer he needed. Anyway, the starting place for his search had to be towards the rear of the Pedlar property — since it was a sure thing that Starbuck and the girl would not have dared risk leaving from the grass along its front — and he judged that the pair would also have left on foot, walking their horses northwards and away from the moon, and wouldn't have risked mounting up and spurring to full gallop until they were at least a quarter of a mile clear of the dwelling. These hints of possible delay braced Kane up; for, what between picking up the treasure from wherever it had been hidden and the footwork that would have been demanded by the first stage of their withdrawal, Starbuck and the blonde were most probably not all that far ahead of him as yet. If he could get a quick start, he ought to be able to overtake the pair by dawn at the latest.

He soon reached the ground towards the rear of the site on which the Pedlar dwelling stood. Here the picket fence continued, but was interrupted at one spot by a five-barred gate. This gate was shut, and could have been so for a long time before that, but the sheriff went into a crouch and began a close examination of the grass across the face of the sealed entrance, spotting muddy scars where the woodwork had recently sagged on weak hinges and ploughed into the wet soil while being dragged aside to allow free passage in or out. But, far more importantly, the area had been imprinted by horseshoes and bootheels and these marks were visible as a trail leading northwards. So it appeared that, as Kane had earlier thought likely, Starbuck and the girl had been heading directly up country when they had left this place. The chances were that they would not deviate from the path of the North Star and that should make pursuing them still easier — especially as, with luck, the captain would not be pushing for maximum speed in his belief that the sheriff had been forced by circumstances to play the constable and was miles behind him making arrests at the Pedlar cottage.

Suddenly Kane's nostrils gave a twitch. He detected a faint but unpleasant stench in the air. The smell was that of vegetable waste and household slops. Kane frowned, and it crossed his mind — as he straightened from his inspection of the earth — that the Aztec treasure, perhaps enclosed in a waterproof bag, could have been sunk in the Pedlar slop pit, which would inevitably exist at the bottom of the late Ivan's back garden, for such a disposal point was common to all country properties of the day.

Did decency put such an idea out of the question? Kane thought not. The smell was too recent and distinctive to ignore. Indeed, the more he thought about it, the more it seemed to him that no better hiding place for a treasure could be devised, for even the most diligent searchers would never dip into filth during their quest and naturally suppose that those who hid things would have the same aversion. Yes, that could be the fact of it. If Starbuck's men — probably among the most experienced of their kind — had searched everywhere on the property and been unable to find what they were looking for, then Ivan Pedlar's hiding place for the jewels had undoubtedly been a most unusual one. Knowing the man, too, Kane could say with certainty that Pedlar — a haunter of the foulest swamps — would have had no compunction about dipping into a slop pit if he had thought that he could keep his secret safe by so doing. Also, the lowest of men were usually the most cunning, and Ivan had certainly not belonged to any superior order of humanity. But none of it mattered much for the moment. He had simply been playing with ideas again. He must still catch his bunny before he could discover for sure how right or wrong he had been.

Then, startled by the abruptness of the noise — for the back door of the nearby cottage burst open and he heard a great shouting of voices from within the dwelling — Kane jerked his mount's head round and started running his horse over the sign that he believed Starbuck and Jill Pedlar had laid down ahead of him. At a guess, he had to accept that the man whom he had knocked senseless at the front of the house had not remained unconscious for as long as he had expected and had no doubt gone running indoors almost at the instant of regaining his senses and created immediate uproar among men virtually shocked out of their sleep with news of an escape that had presaged the discovery of an even greater disaster for them.

Kane kept his head as low as he could, and his horse moving fast at his side. It was bedlam back there now, and it sounded as if all the outlaws had rushed into the open. Kane could hear Colonel Barris's voice, terse and peremptory, shouting above the rest. The colonel had clearly put himself in charge, and there could be no mistake about it. His orders, still fully audible to the swiftly withdrawing sheriff, showed that Barris had a firm grasp of what had happened and was giving the right commands to reduce the damage that the outlaws had already suffered. He was insisting on immediate pursuit, and there was little doubt that all the men present would have headed there and then for the front of the property and the ground on which their horses were waiting, but Kane himself made the vital error that changed all that by catching his right toe on a piece of rock that jutted from the grass underfoot and almost staggering onto his face. The noise carried, and the images of his horse and himself — apparently lost to Barris and company until then against the blackness of the land before them — must have been instantly detected by suddenly straining eyes, for pistols had already begun banging in Kane's direction before the colonel actually called attention to the target and gave the order to open fire.

There was no longer anything to gain by staying afoot. Maximum speed of retreat could be all that mattered to the sheriff now. Spearing his nearside stirrup, Kane heaved into leather, throwing himself forward onto his mount's neck at the instant of arrival and remaining stretched thus as he applied the rowels with vigour. Bullets whimpered past his ears, and horses neighed in fright. Then a slug clipped his cantle, ripping splinters, and steel rang as another tiny missile struck his right stirrup-iron, while he smelled his own hair burning in the moment that hot lead scorched through the thick growth on his nape and passed safely onwards. It was like living in a hail of metal and, missed time and again by no more than the proverbial fraction of an inch, Kane didn't see how he could survive; but he did and, untouched in all that mattered, galloped onwards while what had been the fiercest of fire at his back spluttered out and Colonel Barris renewed his command to run for the horses and give chase.

Picking up his head and shoulders now, Kane let his horse take him along.

The animal had recognised the danger of sudden death back there and was no less fearful of it than he. The mount thundered ahead without any need of prompting, and they covered a good three miles at the same breakneck pace before the creature began to flag a little. Craning, Kane glanced back to where the moonlight lay brightest across the land. He knew Barris and his hunters were there, but he could see nothing of them. Relaxing a trifle, he blew out a cleansing breath. The pursuit didn't amount to much of a threat for the moment. He and his mount had only to keep going and they would totally outrun the riders to their rear in half an hour and then be able to make any turn they wished without the slightest risk of their change of direction being spotted. That would be fine if escape was all that mattered; but, as a hunter himself, his mind had to stay more on what was ahead of him than behind.

While it would be wrong to suggest that he was in any kind of contact with Starbuck and the girl at this moment, he knew that he couldn't be far short — or wide — of them, and he must try to hold his position in relation to that which he imagined they occupied right now. In fact his need was to pinpoint their place upon the land with a minimum of delay, and that would mean climbing high at the first opportunity and taking a look into the country ahead and about him in the hope of glimpsing his quarry while the moon was still above him and bright. The snag of taking an observation was, of course, that a man sitting high could be far more easily spotted by an enemy below him than he could spot a traveller down in the land shadows. Yet the need was there, and things were otherwise as they were, so he would just have to accept the danger involved and not allow himself to be influenced negatively by it.

Almost at once he saw high ground ahead of him and a little to his right. Shifting his mount's jaws the amount necessary, he made for the incline beneath the crest and began climbing steadily. He topped out a few minutes later — aware now that he was riding the western rim of the plateau and stood between River Park and the last stretch of the road back to town. Eyes roving to his left, he allowed his heavily sweating horse to come almost to a halt and have a blow. He wondered for a moment if Starbuck and Jill Pedlar, perhaps anticipating a later pursuit from Rockford could have swung westwards about here — in the hope of throwing the possible hunters off at the start — but he couldn't see what they would have to gain by it, for the Trinity river and Galveston Bay lay beyond the River Park ruin and the road, with its undoubted hazards, could only bring them to Houston and the turn northwards which they had already begun here. No, the pair should be somewhere off his mount's left shoulder at this time and, even if they had heard the recent firing in their wake and judged what it must portend, Kane felt confident that they would not deviate greatly from the course that would take them up into central Texas and the choice of a thousand routes beyond.

Then he spotted the two riders. They were in exactly the area where he had expected them to be, but at a distance which gave them the look of small black toys. They were riding across flats where the rays of the moon reached out and touched their backs every yard of the way. Kane prepared to spur down off his vantage and close in upon the pair below, but then he remembered that Colonel Barris and the members of the Starbuck gang now riding with him must by this time be getting near the place where he had recently left the land beneath and made his climb up here. It would certainly put the kybosh on his night if he went pounding down the slope to his left and straight into the path of those villains.

No, it would be wiser to stay up

here for the time being and watch for those hellions to pass him in the lower gloom. Once placed at the rear of the night's activities, he would not have to worry any longer about protecting his back and would have achieved the best position from which to take full advantage of whatever developments might occur among the enemies ahead of him. After all, he was not the most important character in what was happening tonight, and it was likely that Colonel Barris regarded him as no more than a confounded nuisance; for the colonel and the outlaws were still mainly concerned with getting rich before anything else, and the fact that their lawman quarry had given them the slip would not spoil things for them if they caught up with the traitorous Starbuck and his blonde paramour by way of compensation. 'Horse,' the sheriff said comfortably, bringing his animal to a halt and stepping down, 'I think we should treat ourselves to a little rest. We can spare a couple of minutes. Chew the grass, eh? You've earned it!'

Smiling to himself, Kane fiddled with the butt of his lately appropriated six-shooter, accepting that the fellow who talked to his horse was almost as daft as the guy who spoke to himself, but this plateau was a lonely spot at this hour and the language of the night wind was beyond his understanding. The sound of his own voice seemed the only proof that the world had a material existence and was not just the product of his own over-active imagination. He had done too much thinking this last day.

Events continued in train. There were no surprises. Kane's hunters appeared below and went galloping on northwards, and he remounted when they reached the limit of his vision and then angled down the slope to the west of him and took up the rear position in the chase that he had visualised for himself a short while ago. He went on without pause, but at the kind of three-quarter pace to which he judged the mounts ahead would have been reduced by now — and his own horse could sustain for the rest of the night if it had to — and was again prepared to stick at it for as long as necessary, when the sudden banging of a rifle out of the northern distance caused him to rein back sharply and an answering crackle of gunfire made him further reduce speed.

His horse moving along at no better than a trot now, Kane sank his jaw into another spell of deep thought and could only conclude that Starbuck had unknowingly seen fit to follow his own recent example and climb high to take a look around him by favour of the moon. He must have glimpsed Barris and company on his backtrail and decided that they were getting too close and must be ambushed and at least thinned out.

The captain seemed to be gambling heavily on his skills as a sharpshooter and would be giving all his attention to his grim work. It was also possible that he had forgotten his second enemy when turning to his desperate measure. It could now be Starbuck's turn to watch his back.

# 9

Kane spurred back to full gallop. The shooting ahead of him persisted. The rifle went on dominating crisply, while the answering sixguns produced duller and more booming detonations. Threshing onwards, the sheriff quickly drew nearer to the firing, which he had expected to cease before this — at the withdrawal of the bush-whacker into renewed flight — but it began to seem to him that the exchange had lately altered its character and become more of a pitched battle than some snap shooting by a would-be killer answered by ragged pistol-fire. He was pretty sure that a second rifle was now supporting the first, and he formed the impression that Jill Pedlar must have entered the fray in order to keep Colonel Barris and the other horsemen pinned down. Clearly then, things had not gone as well for Starbuck as he had undoubtedly hoped — with fewer casualties among his pursuers than he had expected — and, at a guess, that had placed him in the position where further retreat was being made more and more difficult. In fact Kane wondered if Starbuck had misjudged his attempted delaying action disastrously; for, with a soldier of Barris's tactical experience against him, he could soon end up being encircled and destroyed. Kane was amazed that matters could so swiftly have come to this pass; for at one stage back there he had had the feeling that Starbuck had dared and was going to get away with his daring. He might still, of course — for the sheriff's reading of what was happening before him could be at fault in all sorts of ways — but, in the general perception of it, Starbuck's ultimate success began to seem a lot less likely.

It wasn't long before Kane saw gunflashes ahead. Slowing his horse, he gazed narrowly towards the area of the land beyond him where the fight was taking place and soon formed the impression that the rifles were blazing down from the top of a rock mass that dominated the path overland which the chase had been following. Indeed, it could almost be said that Colonel Barris and company had been galloping into the jaws of death when Starbuck had opened fire on them. The captain and Jill Pedlar appeared to be shooting from an excellent position — and had there been more of them they might well have held out indefinitely and finally whittled their attackers away to almost nothing — but, as it was, they were the ones under threat from numbers and appeared vulnerable on their left, where a boulder-strewn grade offered their enemies the chance of creeping up past the captain's vantage and eventually firing down on him and the girl from a position higher than their own.

Again insofar as Kane could be

certain of what was being organised where the guns were flashing, that part of it looked dangerous indeed for Starbuck and the blonde, since there were enough of the outlaws present to allow for a portion of the gang keeping the rifles busy with frontal fire while the remainder of the badmen began creeping up the incline to the east of the captain's firing point. Yet the breaking up of a body also meant the weakening of its parts and, taking in the lie of the land and the fact that the men yonder were hardly expecting any interference from him, Kane felt reasonably certain that he could turn what seemed to be happening over the way to his own advantage. There could be the devil of a risk in it all right — and he was probably mad to consider what he had in mind — but the element of surprise was never to be underestimated, and he reckoned that, if he could sneak above the climbing outlaws before they could gain the height they needed, he ought to be able to shoot several of them before they realized what was happening.

The idea was basically sound, yet the sheriff hesitated. While he had guts enough for most things, he was not exactly suicidal, and he had no good feeling inside him about what he was teetering into — especially as the old argument that he was operating outside his jurisdiction was valid again — but he was into this business now about as deeply as he could get and felt a stern compulsion to see it through. Everything had come together here, and he must not let it break up and the pieces be separated again. He was one man against very large odds, but the gamble could be worth it. As he visualised the matter, if he did his duty and took out a fair part of the outlaw gang, there was a good chance that the other elements in the situation would reduce or eliminate the remainder and leave him with no more than a cleaning up job. Or at least the kind of fight at the last which he could manage. Yes, he must try it.

He moved in a little closer to the guns. Then, about three hundred yards short of the battle — where the risk of being spotted became pronounced — he turned his horse into a pool of shadow and dismounted. After that he dived away to his right and started climbing the slope which he could see a cluster of outlaws tackling elsewhere. There were plenty of boulders on the grade and, choosing the biggest ones to shelter him where he could, he kicked and scrambled into the ascent, moving upwards at a pace as fast as any that he could have ever achieved. Far outstripping the men climbing on his left, he reached the ground just beneath the summit of this particular rise and then squared round to face the area for which they were making. Then, his feet scampering again, he threaded the obstructions of the upper rockland and reached a position which commanded the section of the acclivity up which the villains were ascending. Halting, he drew himself fully erect and jerked his revolver, aiming down the incline before him. It was time to start shooting, and to take full advantage of the surprise that he was about to cause, but he found that he could not open fire on the wrongdoers without warning them first — as the law required of him — and it was in his most forbidding voice that he yelled: 'Drop the hoglegs, you bastards, or take snuff!'

The climbers stopped instantly. They stood gazing up at him, and Kane heard dirt and pebbles sliding out behind their checked heels in the silence that expressed the shock of the moment. Then a voice which he believed to be that of ex-Sergeant Major Abel Sweetman shouted: 'It's that son-of-a-bitch lawman again! Plug him, boys!'

Kane covered the speaker and let fly. Down went his man, but another stepped up and took the place of the first, shooting back. Braced to receive fire, the sheriff triggered again. His target could as well have been punched by a giant as shot with a

Colt forty-four. The outlaw spun like a top off the shelf which had been supporting him and then went head-over-heels down the slope at his back. He took a comrade with him and the man began screaming in fright as he vanished from the lawman's sight in the kind of speeding tumble which would surely carry him back to the flat ground off which his climb had commenced.

'Kill him before he can do any more damage!' boomed Alonzo Barris's refined tones from below. 'You have your chance! Make an end of him now!'

The exhortation seemed to have the desired effect. Shadowy figures came charging up and onwards, their sixguns flashing redly. Still straight of back and taking his time about it, Kane fired at the members of the onset off an extended arm. He dropped first one of his enemies and then another, and the clinical accuracy of his shooting so discouraged the remaining outlaws in the bunch that they turned about and fled, taking the slope below in frantic bounds and skips, while Kane felled another one of their number with a carefully aimed fifth bullet, recognising his victim's death cry as Tony Essen's.

'You cowards!' Colonel Barris bawled contemptuously from the foot of the ascent. 'Get back up there and fight! He is only one man!'

The fact of it was too self-evident to be denied, but a snarling voice soon told the colonel what he could do with himself and — it seemed to the downward peering Kane — Barris was so incensed by what he had heard that he shot the villain who had insulted him without more ado.

'Who's the coward now, you Yankee murderer!' the sheriff shouted down at the colonel, absolutely fuming at the callousness of what he believed had just occurred. 'You climb up here and face me! But you lack the guts yourself when last comes to last!'

'I'll remember that, Sheriff!' Barris

declared. 'You'll find me ready, willing, and able when the time comes! But don't play me for a fool!'

'No need!' Kane responded, his meaning all too clear.

'How dare you!' the colonel roared, again mildly put out.

'Yeah, how dare you?' Captain Starbuck's voice now echoed as mockingly as Kane's own from the top of his vantage, which the sheriff could make out some thirty degrees to his right and about fifty feet below him. 'You can't talk to one of our honoured vanquishers like that! This is how you talk to them!' And his rifle cracked out.

Colonel Barris uttered a great cry of pain, and Kane heard the thud of the big Yankee's body striking the ground.

'Got him!' Starbuck chortled viciously. 'Now it's your turn, Sheriff.'

'Like hell it is!' Kane contradicted, and he blasted off the final bullet in his cylinder towards the man whom he could see raised up and aiming at him off the summit of the outcrop that stood foul at the base of the slope adjacent.

Starbuck jerked backwards, obviously hit, and Kane broke open the loading gate on his Colt and tipped the barrel of his weapon skywards, showering the rock at his feet with spent shells as he spun the pistol's cylinder and then dived for the cartridges in his gunbelt to make an at least partial reload of the revolver before the captain could make any sort of recovery and come up to scratch again. But he had yet to fumble his first bullet into place, when a movement over to his right and level with his shoulder caught his eye. 'Jill?' he questioned, pretty sure that it was a woman's shape that he could see through the shadows at the top of the slope, where a kind of bridge connected Starbuck's vantage with the ground which he himself commanded. 'What the dickens are you about, girl? Give it up right now! I may still be able to get you off with a caution — or a light sentence at worst!'

'Sorry, Adam!' she said. 'This is all or nothing — and I wouldn't have it any other way!'

'Don't talk such — ' Kane began protesting; but flame darted at him from the muzzle of the girl's rifle and something that felt like a blacksmith's hammer struck him above the left ear, and his light instantly began failing. For a split second he was aware of falling, but he didn't feel himself hit the ground; and that seemed to be it.

He came slowly to himself in due course, his consciousness rising out of a pit of total blackness. Yet the darkness on which he opened his eyes was only a little less complete than that inside himself, and the pain of which he now became aware within his brain made him wish that he had actually died when Jill Pedlar had shot at him. Better to have all your head torn away than just half of it. Perhaps he had recovered his senses only to die.

With his luck, it could easily turn out like that.

Using his hands to thrust the weight of his torso off the ground, Kane made an immense effort and tipped himself into a sitting position. Holding his temples between his fingers now, he shut his eyes again as the black, black world came swooping at him. He felt absolutely awful — sick, dizzy, and cold to the bone. Damn that Jill! He'd smack her backside for this one when he caught her. If he caught her. How long had he been unconscious? An hour? Two? Three? Six months or a year? Perhaps eternity had run its course while he lay upon this slope, and the Almighty had set off on another round. No. Those stars that were now peeping through above him were all too familiar, and the feeling of being wet — which seemed to be the reason for his being so cold — was special to Adam Kane, and would never be quite the same in anybody else.

Kane raised himself slowly to his

feet. The silence under the ridge had a hollow and brooding quality about it. He could smell wet earth underfoot. It had been raining not so long ago. But hadn't he thought it unlikely that the district would get through the night without another rainstorm? The brightness of the Gulf moon had always been as false as the bustle on a French whore. So far as the sheriff could tell, it had rained down in torrents — and most of it had fallen on him. Now he gently touched himself above the left ear. There was a small wound present, but it was nothing to get alarmed about, though the bump on which it lay was big enough. It had been a near thing, but he had in fact been merely winged. If Jill Pedlar's bullet had travelled an inch further to the left, it would have been all up with him. As it was, he'd be almost as good as new by the end of the week — always supposing, of course, that somebody didn't do him more and worse harm in the meantime.

The sheriff realized that he had dropped his gun when he had fallen. Kneeling, he stretched out a hand and felt about on the damp rock and soil around him. After several moments of this activity, he came upon the weapon and picked it up. Then he returned to the vertical once more and reloaded the empty Colt with another lot of cartridges taken from the loops on his gunbelt. After that, with his fingers tightly shut on the pistol's butt, he stood and gazed uncertainly into a night that now seemed to be flickering with the faint grey light of the false dawn. He was conscious that he had no reliable idea of how the gun battle had finished here, and knew that he must go and discover as nearly as he could how matters had come out before he attempted anything else.

There was an important question that he kept asking himself. How badly had he wounded Jack Starbuck? The captain had almost certainly taken the bullet which Kane had shot at him in the upper body, and the probability was that he had been severely hurt. There was even the chance that his body was lying atop the firing perch nearby. Better go and look.

Gathering himself, Kane moved off to his right and made his way across the face of the slope to where the bridge that linked it with the vantage which dominated the lower ground was located. Walking over the slightly arched path which joined the main incline and the outcrop together, he reached what had been Starbuck's firing position. The man's body was not there and, lacking any form of light by which to see bloodstains or other evidence of how badly the captain had been wounded, Kane had to accept that the man had survived the fight in good enough shape to continue his journey up country with Jill Pedlar. But that was about what he had expected, and he allowed himself no more than a grimace of regret over the additional energy that he would soon have to expend in catching up with them again. At least they would now suppose him dead, and it was likely that they would not be worrying too much about pursuers any more, since he was fairly sure that Colonel Barris was defunct — or at least out of the chase — and that any survivors among the outlaws were probably too lacking in will and intelligence to continue hunting down a treasure that was so far outside their normal conception of loot. And what was even more to the point they knew how well their erstwhile boss could shoot. Still, permutations did remain and the sheriff perceived that he must continue to watch the details.

Bearing this in mind, he withdrew from Starbuck's shooting platform and returned to the spot across the way from which he had himself fired down on Amos Sweetman and the other badmen who had attacked him in force while charging up the climb, and he slowly descended, locating and checking bodies on his way. There were no wounded among the fallen, and this enabled him to reach the base of the slope without much delay en route. Moving on the level once more, he came upon two more bodies while groping around, but neither man was Colonel Barris and the slight optimism which he had previously felt began to dilute as he questioned himself intently as to what had taken place just here.

He had literally heard the colonel fall after receiving Starbuck's rifle shot. The man had gone down with quite a thump. It had been easy to imagine him lying dead. Yet had he, like the sheriff — for amazing coincidences daily occurred — received only some form of glancing wound from Starbuck's long gun which had allowed him to get up in due course and set off on the captain's trail again? It might seem unlikely, but it was possible. The only other feasible explanation was that Barris's body, dead or wounded, had been carried away by others to be looked after.

But, knowing the utter selfishness of the outlaw breed, Kane could think of no circumstances that could have arisen among the wrongdoers that might have spurred them to an action at once so altruistic and arduous. No, here was another of those disagreeable things which sometimes had to be accepted. Colonel Barris was still out there — active in whatever degree — and it appeared that he must still figure in the reckoning to come. Between his chilled flesh and sickening headache, Kane shivered anew at the thought of it. The devil had surely set his foot tonight!

The sheriff walked back to the area in which he had earlier left his horse. He found the animal cropping placidly and quite indifferent to his reappearance. Hell might have broken loose nearby, but the animal didn't care. Its attitude seemed to suggest that people set too much importance by their lives and human affairs, and that, for Kane, seemed to put his recent doings into a truer perspective. What did his strivings add up to? He was just a guy doing a job. Hadn't he told himself as much before? If he did his work well, the US Treasury might benefit somewhat, and if he did it badly the good folk of Rockford would take away his star. Heaven would not fall or the earth rise in glory. Even the greatest deeds were of little worth in the great flux of time. He was just another visitor passing through, and the only worth in anything was what he put there himself. But the satisfaction of a job well done was only found when a man had invested everything he had to give in futility. Life was full of little catches — wasn't it just! Yet life had no alternative, and the only thing to do was get on with it.

Kane swung into his saddle. Then he let his horse know all about it. He pushed the animal to full gallop and kept it there. Past Starbuck's shooting perch he thundered and then onwards. To hell with Colonel Barris! He had only contempt for that Yankee varmint right now. It was the captain he wanted. The man who had turned a nice girl like Jill Pedlar into a potential murderess. No doubt the varmint had claimed her innocence too. Once a girl had lost that, she let go of the rest and might become anything. Lord — but he was having some thoughts tonight, wasn't he? 'Giddup!' he bawled at his mount, the rowels striking deep. 'I'll sell you down in Mexico if I hear much more about it!'

The day was emerging. Uneven spirals of light misted upwards above the long shadow of the land and spread into the grey vapours of the east. Kane seemed to be in the middle of nowhere and heading past the same. Then a seabird cried above him in a reminder that he was still well short of twenty miles beyond the Gulf. Now true light came and distances dissolved into distance, and the echoing immensity of the morning stunned the sheriff's tired wits. This couldn't go on; his horse was done in and so was he. But what was true for them was true for the other participants in this madness too. Add, also, that Starbuck was wounded — perhaps unto death — and something had to break before long.

Kane let his mount slow beneath him. It was still game enough, but crossing sand, and its hooves bit deep and held, a recipe for exhaustion if ever there was one. They kept going at a steady rate but little more. Now the sun peeped, and there was glory in the morning, yellow and bright, and Kane saw cacti between cow-grass and river brakes. It appeared to him that he was travelling a miniature desert which ran like a dun stripe through this land of many waters, with rocky outcrops where sight dimmed up front and a ruin standing in isolation upon the middle ground.

There it was, the Mission of Santa Marguerita, almost as old as the Spanish Conquest itself and unfrequented from one year to the next these days by all save the ravens and the foxes. He had known of its presence, but forgotten about it, though he should have realized its significance as the only place of shelter around. Then, glancing about him almost as quickly as the thought had come, he made out tracks in the sand over to his left that were almost as new as his own and saw that they were heading for the tumbledown church. The imprints could hardly have been churned up by anybody but his quarry, and meant that he would probably find Jack Starbuck and Jill Pedlar in the ruined mission. The pair could not be anticipating a follower, and the surprise was his to spring. Suddenly he was wide awake again and ready for anything. But he prayed that those two fools — if he did come upon them here — would not force him to shoot. He had spilled more than enough blood in recent hours.

Kane kept moving parallel with the

hoofprint on his left, and he was watchful in the last degree as he neared the crumbling mission — which was a typical Spanish church of its time and built of adobe and plaster, with a roof of red tiles and a bell-tower standing above the main door — but he sensed no movement in or around the place and, coming to the low outcrop of sandstone on which the structure had been founded, he could see no sign that horses had recently stopped at the front of the building or anybody entered it at that point.

In fact lifting his eyes northwards in the still early light, he could discern where twin lines of hoofmarks reappeared in the sandy going beyond the mission's foundation rock and then pursued a shallow curve in the same direction and only vanished where the flatness of the land smoothed out all detail on its surface. It seemed to him — and he felt a sense of disappointment because of it — that he had made the error of taking an enemy's intention for granted, since it seemed that Starbuck and the girl had not been actually seeking the mission of Santa Marguerita or had any intention of entering it. Yet that was not really so remarkable, for they were still fairly close to home and might still have a guilty fear of pausing while the chance remained that something further could go wrong.

Brow furrowing, the sheriff sucked his teeth thoughtfully. Reading another's mind was always difficult when stress was involved. So why bother with it? The sign was there upon the ground, and plain enough to see. He had only to follow it. But why in heaven's name would two riders drift in close enough to the ruined mission to lose the marks of their passage on the foundation rock of the place before veering back to pick up their original line of travel beyond? True, there was no reason why they shouldn't — and it could be argued that they slightly speeded up their progress for a hundred yards or more on the solid going across the ruin's front — but, ever the sceptic, Kane wasn't quite convinced by his own reasoning and, drawing rein, dismounted on impulse and stalked over to the mission door. Gripping the iron ring to which the latch was attached, he twisted hard and pushed inwards. The door opened with a groan, but evenly enough on hinges that were still good and he saw at once the spread of sand which had drifted in under the woodwork when the east wind blew and now carried the fresh impress of male and female boot-soles. So here was proof, then, that Jack Starbuck and Jill Pedlar had entered not so long ago. He had been right to check up where the detective in him doubted.

He pushed the door open as far as it would go. This allowed the morning light to stream down the length of the church as it probably hadn't done for a century or more. He advanced slowly down the central aisle, passing the chipped and leaning font on his left and seeing a picture of decay everywhere else — from the rotting pews on either hand right up to the altar. Here the termites had long ago chewed the wooden crucifix into collapsed pieces, while the altar cloths were in tatters and the boards underfoot broken through and tilted up. Nothing of value remained, of course, and the severity of the Jesuit mind was apparent all around in the right-angled simplicity of the screen, cornices, and window-spaces, but Kane could still feel a lingering holiness present and he crossed himself almost unawares, retreating from the altar rails with his head bowed. And thus he would have left the church but, as he drew level with the font again, a faint stench impinged upon his nostrils and this took him back several hours to when, crouched in the moonlight near the rest of Ivan Pedlar's cottage, he had detected that bad smell which had made him wonder whether Jill and the captain had recovered the Aztec treasure from a hiding place in the household slop pit.

Nostrils still twitching, the sheriff first confirmed to himself that the remembered stench was indeed real and that he wasn't imagining it, and then he started tracking it — spitting a time or two as he went — and within a few moments he was crouched beside the foot of the font in the certainty that the foul smell was issuing from beneath it. Realizing that he would have to tip up the base of the font in order to peer under it, he studied the stone column which supported the christening basin. It looked sound enough, despite the damage done it by time and impious hands, and Kane put his shoulder to the already slightly canted shaft and pushed with all his strength, getting the power of his back and leg muscles into the exercise, and the font tipped away from him and revealed beneath it an aperture which contained a canvas bag with wooden handles that closely resembled similar bags of the carpet type. Here then, almost certainly, was Professor James Firman's treasure of the Lone Star, and the stench of vegetable water and human waste upon it was enough to make Kane feel sick at the stomach.

This had to be done. The sheriff reached down with his left hand and lifted the bag out of its resting place. Then he set it aside and, gradually backing away from the position in which he was propping the tilted font up, he let the piece of stonework settle to rest again and stepped back from its base, straightening up once more and breathing deeply from the strain. He felt hugely pleased with what he had just done — yet, strangely enough, also felt a twinge of wry sympathy for his departed quarry. Starbuck and Jill Pedlar had clearly divested themselves of the treasure to facilitate their own movements and to keep it safe until they could recover it at some future date that was more fortunate to their affairs; but they had no sooner made the effort and taken the risk involved than he had come along and brought all their scheming to nothing. It was remarked every day that the devil was a bad paymaster, and here indeed was further proof of it.

Kane picked up the canvas bag and carried it outside. In a sense he considered his job done — though he must still do everything he could to catch the thieves — but he could not forbear to look into the bag, so he parted the wooden handles and opened its top. Inside sure enough were those one hundred pieces of Aztec jewellery that comprised the famous treasure, though the hoard looked a rough and tawdry one just then. The diamond, emerald, and sapphire necklaces were covered with dust and the gems had no depth or glitter about them, while the silver diadems and such were tarnished and appeared worthless, as did the rings, bracelets, medallions and other items present. In fact under this pristine light the treasure seemed exposed as the symbol of human covetousness and the delusion of riches. There was infinitely more worth in a healthy body and three square meals a day than in this tangle of odds-and-ends which had been extracted at such great pains from Mother Earth and shaped with more of the same by ancient jewelsmiths. Yes, call it a fortune if you liked, but the US Treasury would be more than welcome to it as far as the sheriff was concerned. He shut the bag with a decisive movement, and was about to lift and carry it to his horse, when a rifle banged distantly and a bullet thudded into the mission wall several feet to his left.

It seemed that his halt at the church had been watched from the first. But what had that rifle shot been trying to tell him? For he was sure that no effort to kill him had just been made.

# 10

Moving up to his horse, Kane attached the canvas bag containing the Aztec treasure to his pommel. Then he stood gazing into the northwest across his animal's back. He was more or less certain that the recent shot had come in from that direction, and he scanned the ground up to half a mile beyond him with the narrowed eye of absolute concentration. All at once the tiniest of movements plucked at his attention. He believed that he had seen a doubled body dodging from one runnel to the next — the slight folds in the land which were obviously out there being invisible to him as such at this distance — and he came to the conclusion, as his gaze once more picked up a crouched figure for a split second, that he was watching the retreat of Jill Pedlar from her firing position of a minute ago. Clearly his enemies had had him under observation for much longer than he had supposed from the instant of the shot cracking out, and that Starbuck and the girl had recognised him readily enough after they had perceived themselves at some point in the recent past to have a pursuer again. It must have been a nasty shock for them, and perhaps made them wonder if he was one of these men who was obviously not destined to die by violence — if such a being genuinely existed — and now they were trying to deal with him again as best they could.

The sheriff was pretty confident that Jill Pedlar wanted him to follow her. Was she trying to create some kind of diversion? — lead him up her rifle sights into a bushwhacking? — or simply draw him into some place yonder where she could accost him and talk? He felt the last of the three. Did she intend to invite him into taking a share of the Firman collection and then joining up with Starbuck and herself? It was the sort of crazy offer that criminals often made when nearing the end of their tether. There was even the possibility that the pair had planted the bag of treasure under the font in the expectation that he would find it — as a form of bait in fact — but, while that notion could make a kind of sense, he couldn't really credit it. Jill Pedlar knew him better than that, and he felt instinctively that the treasure had been hidden to remain so until Starbuck and the girl had completed their present purpose and could pick it up again. No, altogether, though the captain and the blonde might be nearing the end of their wits they were still not thinking in quite the defeated terms which had lately crossed his mind. They were scheming again, he'd swear it, though he was completely mystified on this occasion by how they were trying to deceive him. Kane sighed heavily to himself. This business was going to go hard right up to the bitter end, and he guessed he'd better stay watchful but play along for the moment. Sooner or later Jill and her captain would make an error which would betray their true purpose — because there were all manner of things here that didn't really stand up to the immediate test of logic.

Now Kane remounted his horse. He spurred off northwestwards across the desert strip towards the spot where he had last glimpsed Jill Pedlar. He arrived in the general area a couple of minutes later. After that he began casting around for the blonde or her sign. Almost at once he spotted footmarks in the sand. These led him on, but promised only to deceive, for they brought him to an expanse of shallowly outcropping rock which appeared to be several hundred acres in extent, and there he lost the trace, which he was forced to suppose had been the girl's intentions after all. However, he had his luck a short while later when he came upon a pile of fresh horse droppings in a small depression which revealed where Jill's mount had stood while she was roving further afield with her Winchester, and he decided that he would search for new signs of her on her probable line of withdrawal northwards. He should be able to spare the time to travel a mile or two on the off-chance without losing out completely in the process.

He went clattering off across the field of stone before him at a steady canter. Soon he came to ground where sand and grass mingled and clumps of cactus also had a place. Here he lighted on the new trace which he had been seeking, and followed its rather skimpy presence for about a mile before losing it again. Only a short way after that the outcrop ended and he saw before him a spread of rough pasture that tilted upwards to the east of the spot and cut a dark edge against the sky. He discovered on climbing this ground that it brought him to a river scene that wound southwards from here onwards towards the stretches of waterside grass and timber which his straining eyes had detected wide of him and to the east while he was approaching the ruined mission.

It looked very well, but his interest still lay to the north of him, where the fugitives would have an ever-increasing expanse of country into which to manoeuvre out of his path. It was about now, however, that the obvious came home to him once more. He had been supposing, ever since setting out in pursuit of Jill Pedlar about half an hour ago, that she was riding with the intention of catching up with a still fleeing Starbuck somewhere ahead of her, but he realized now that during this latest stage of the chase he had nowhere seen any trace of a second horse on the ground that he was covering.

So intent had Kane been on the chase itself that he had missed the plain fact that Starbuck and the blonde had separated. Now he came to consider it, nothing could have been more deliberate. Jill could only be leading him away from the wounded Starbuck, whose condition must have deteriorated to the extent that he could no longer keep up with her or have any hope of staying ahead of a future spurt by the persistent lawman. Yes, he had been easily deceived by that clever girl; she had led him to this furthest point east and completely astray. Then, with that much accomplished, it figured she had slanted off north-westwards and would be hammering onwards at full gallop to join up with Starbuck again on some previously decided course. The sheriff cursed himself in disgust. It had come to a rare pass when a girl whom he had supposed to be empty-headed had had the best of him!

He rode down from the edge above the river. After that he retraced his ride to the limits of the nearer extent of outcropping rock. It would have been from about here that Jill had angled away west of north. Once more he began casting around him. Then, almost stopped at a space where the soil was deep, he saw hoofprints which had unquestionably been made by the blonde's slender-legged mount. But the trouble was the tracks weren't heading in the right direction. They were moving southwards. That damned female had him puzzled anew! What reason could she have for riding back towards the sea? It didn't make sense. Or — did it?

What if Jill Pedlar was quite simply heading for home — because Jack Starbuck, turned back in the same direction across the west was heading there too? A wounded man who was badly in need of treatment would require a bed to lie upon and a regular supply of clean water and medicines. It got worse and worse the more he thought about it. Those two had bamboozled him so totally that he could have spent the rest of today — and perhaps more time tomorrow, as the guide to a county posse — chasing his tail in this neighbourhood while Jill and the captain were resting up in comparative safety far removed from the action. If the girl hadn't got a trifle careless at this spot — and given him the vital clue to the couple's true intentions — he might never have dreamed what they were up to and remained in ignorance when they had left Pedlar's Claw again, starting virtually from scratch, and begun their second ride northwards, no doubt with the idea of recovering the treasure which they had concealed at the ruined mission and then journeying onwards as they had planned before. Yet, as Kane saw it now, their craft hadn't ended even there; for, if the worst had come to the worst — while they were anywhere within the county jurisdiction but had had no actual evidence of robbery about them — they could probably have ensured Jill's freedom from prosecution and her continued ability to recover the Aztec treasure and hold on to it until such time as the captain — who had too many crimes to his name to avoid jail — could get paroled or make his escape from behind bars. He doubted that Starbuck and the blonde had missed a trick, but their plotting had finally come unstuck now and nothing could save them. Yet he still had much to do before he could call this job finished.

The sheriff pointed his mount's head southwards. He let the horse feel his rowels but didn't press for more than half speed. He was in no hurry to bring the blonde in sight, and would be quite content to make the ride back a few miles in her wake. What he did intend to do, though, as soon as he came to the high ground to the east of the Trinity river — which more or less connected the River Park grounds with Rockford — was turn aside and climb to its summit. He would then approach the swamps of Pedlar's Claw along the western edge of the plateau. If the girl should halt along the way and take a hard look behind her, he would be riding above her field of vision and she would be given no reason to doubt that her final ploy had succeeded and that she had left him far behind her in a state of bafflement.

He settled down to the ride. It was just a matter now of enduring another spell in the saddle. Not that the simple act of riding was in any sense onerous at this hour of the morning. The breeze was a cool one and meeting him straight off the sea, and the sun was not yet high enough to dazzle or enervate. He should be back at Pedlar's Claw before the real heat of the day began drawing sweat. So he kept bumping onwards, made his climb when he came to it, then followed the ridge southwards and entered the long descent towards the swamplands, with the woods on his left and the white shape of Jill Pedlar's home on his right.

To limit any possible view of his approach from the windows of the cottage, Kane veered out to the west — once off the descent — and closed in upon the dwelling with eyes watchful and a check on his mount. He looked for horses standing outside the property, but saw no sign of any beast around and felt a sudden surge of doubt about having returned here, though he suppressed it instantly, since it went almost without saying that — assuming their safe arrival before his own — Jill and Starbuck would immediately have hidden their horses in the Pedlar stables. Nevertheless, the place did have a dead air about it and the sheriff's inner disquiet refused to be entirely quelled as he rode right up to the northern length of the property's picket fencing and gazed across the garden at the kitchen door through which he had escaped from the house the night before.

Halting, Kane stepped down. Then he raised his left leg over the fence and swung the other to join it on the garden beyond. Now he walked across the dug ground to the door. Raising the latch, he gave the woodwork the tiniest of shoves and the way in opened to him, the hinges hardly murmuring. Then he stepped indoors and paused in the heavy silence beyond the threshold. After that he peered around the room in which he was standing, gaze seeking any traces of recently renewed occupation, but everything appeared to him much as it had been when the light had faded the previous evening — with the obvious difference, of course, that Jill Pedlar's severed bonds lay under the bucket which had been suspended above the place where she had lain to play its part in the Chinese water torture. His own still partially knotted bonds were also lying where he had kicked them off. The memory of it all was still there, yet already fading, for it seemed to him that an age of succeeding events had by now all but buried the great deception which Jill Pedlar and Jack Starbuck had practised on everybody else in the cottage the night before.

The sheriff drew his revolver. Then, catfooting, he moved across the kitchen and listened at the parlour door.

No sound reached him through the woodwork. Easing his way into the living room, he once more sent his gaze darting around him — seeking the same fresh signs as before that the place was again being lived in — but once again there was no detail of any kind present to arouse a greater caution in him than he was already showing. As a matter of fact, though, Starbuck and his gang had turned this room into something of a pigsty and left it the same. It was possible that a returning Jill had looked at it and then turned her back in despair. Perhaps she and the captain had gone to bed. Kane yawned profoundly at the luxury of the thought. He could do with a few hours' shut-eye himself, and they could be in no better case. At least he had lain unconscious for a few hours — if that could be counted as rest in any true meaning of the word.

Now the sheriff tiptoed into the further corner of the room on his right. There was a door set in the wall to the right of this angle which gave access to a bedroom that he knew to be the main sleeping place in the cottage. Once more he reached out and depressed a latch, and again a door opened softly in front of him. Pushing the woodwork back as far as it would go, he left it standing so and crossed the threshold fully, letting out a little grunt of shocked surprise, for on the bed directly before him — lying in the light that entered through a window set in the room's back wall to the left of the bed — lay Captain Jack Starbuck himself. The man had been stretched out precisely and his limbs straightened the same. His eyes were closed as if in sleep, but his face was just beginning to relax into the peaceful grin of death. His chest showed why he had died, for there was a bullet-hole in his blood-soaked shirt just below the spot where the cloth covered his left pectoral. The sheriff's slug had hit him hard last night — which came as no real surprise to Kane — and he had been booked for hell from the instant that the slug had pierced him.

Kane stepped up to the dead man and touched his right hand. The warmth of life was still present in Starbuck's long fingers. That meant he could not have been dead for an hour yet. Probably he had reached the cottage at the end of a tortured ride back, lain himself down, and expired almost at once. Well, he had been a fine-looking guy — though the world was a heap the better for his loss — and he had perhaps been lucky to cash in as easily as he appeared to have done. But now he was must answer for his sins to a higher court than any in Texas. Not least of them would be the wrong that he had done Jill Pedlar, for corruption of the soul was probably the worst crime of them all in the statutes of heaven.

The sheriff glanced round him. Where was that girl? She had clearly been here, and couldn't be far away. In that tree-house of hers, perhaps? Most likely. Well, he'd have to go and find her. Sighing, he thrust his pistol away. He didn't feel there'd be any further trouble. The girl had more sense than to brace him, he was sure.

He sensed rather than saw the shadow that flitted across the parlour at his back. Blinking to himself, and uncertain about it, he spun round, trying to assess what had actually occurred. Then he picked up a whisper of rapid footfalls from the kitchen. Whatever else, he was sure those tiny sounds were real enough. 'Jill!' he bawled peremptorily, perceiving that the girl must have been hiding in her own bedroom until a moment ago and simply seized the opportunity to escape while his back was turned. Dammit! It seemed that he had got it wrong again. She was going to give him further trouble. 'Jill!' he yelled a second time, adding: 'Quit it — or I'll give it to you!'

There was no response. Kane let rip with an oath that did him no credit. Then he went in pursuit of the blonde. Across the parlour he chased full pelt, through the kitchen he dived headlong, and out of the back door he charged, leaping to the middle of the garden patch in time to see the blonde Jill already astride his horse and taking out northwards in rare style — a hand resting significantly on that stinking canvas bag which held jewels worth a huge fortune — but she had travelled only a few yards, when a gun spoke somewhere not far to her left and the bullet from it swept her out of the saddle and sent her spinning head-over-heels across the turf when she hit the ground.

Kane didn't wait to see how she fetched up. He had already turned in the direction of the rifle which had so abruptly ended her flight. There could only be one answer to what had happened, and there, sitting his great battle horse at the edge of the late Ivan Pedlar's back garden, was Alonzo Barris. Now the colonel set steel to hide and sent his mount dashing towards the mount that he had just denuded of its rider. The animal had virtually stopped, with the sudden loss of the girl from its back, and it was plain that Barris meant to catch up its reins and speed away with the creature trailing behind his own — thus robbing the sheriff of any chance of starting an immediate pursuit. Kane was outraged! The sheer cheek of that blue-bellied bastard! He'd pay Alonzo Barris for this — just see if he didn't! The man must have followed him here!

Up to the picket fence he ran, and over it he jumped — lunging on beyond the palings to grab the tail of Barris's horse. His fingers seized hard, and the arrival of his weight at the mount's rear acted as a considerable braking force. In fact this pull, coupled to the checking movements which the colonel had been forced to make at his mount's head in order to render it possible for him to bend over the animal's withers and gather up the reins of the horse which he was seeking to take in tow, had so much further reduced the freedom of movement which Barris's mount needed that it neighed in anger and reared perceptibly at the restraint. Shouting his own rage and frustration, as he perceived that things were about to go wrong, the colonel craned round and slashed at Kane with the barrel of his rifle, but the sheriff had anticipated this counter and was already ducking and the swinging bore passed over the top of his head, missing by inches. Barris was thrown completely off balance and, before he could recover from the sweep and set himself to try again, Kane seized him round the middle and hauled him out of his saddle, literally hurling him sideways to the ground.

The big man hit the earth with enough force to send a shudder through the surrounding soil, but managed to retain his senses and his hold upon his Winchester. He attempted to do something dangerous with the rifle, but the sheriff tore it out of his grasp and pitched it into the back garden of the Pedlar home. Then he grabbed the colonel by the lapels of his coat and stood him upright, banging in a series of short rights to the ex-soldier's solar plexus. Time and again his fist sank inches deep into the other's flesh. Barris sagged and let out strange whooping noises as the air was driven out of his lungs, but he began fending at his opponent as best he could and further maddened Kane by giving him a bloody nose.

The sheriff brushed what amounted to Barris's token defence aside and punched the colonel round in a circle, banging blow after blow against the big man's chin and finally dropping him with an uppercut which he screwed in from the right, starting the punch from the level of his enemy's hip and passing his bunched knuckles under Barris's left armpit. The colonel was clearly beaten — if he had ever had a chance indeed — but, against the expectation, a fear that showed itself in his eyes brought him to his feet and he threw himself at the lawman, trying to bear him down with his greatly superior body mass; but Kane merely side-stepped his enemy's elephantine rush and, drawing back his left leg to provide the prop he needed, made another twist of his torso and swung over a right that detonated behind the floundering colonel's left ear with the kind of force that might have stunned a far stronger man than he. This time Barris fell on his face and lay inert.

Doubting that his man was actually senseless, the sheriff bent at the colonel's side and removed the other's revolver from its holster, hurling the weapon in much the same direction as Barris's rifle had gone a minute or so before. Then, kicking a foot under the big man, Kane heaved him over onto his back and stood looking down into his battered face. Panting, the sheriff felt little more than satisfaction now, for he had expended the worst of his fury in the hiding which he had handed the

Yankee. 'Get up!' he breathed, stirring the colonel with a none too gentle toe. 'You're going to prison, mister, and it will be my pleasure to provide the testimony that puts you there. For the rest of your natural, I hope!'

Barris spat blood, but remained on the ground, perhaps wisely. 'You vengeful rebel scum!' he mouthed bitterly.

'Oh, I'm vengeful all right,' Kane acknowledged, 'and I'm a rebel sure enough. As for the scum — ? Well, my fine sir, the worst of our Southern scum always proved itself superior to your Northern gentry!' He stabbed a finger right straight between the colonel's eyes. 'Now you keep your lip tight buttoned and lie quiet — or I'll set about you again. And next time I won't know when to stop!'

Kane swung away from Barris in utter disdain. He went reeling over to where Jill Pedlar lay on the grass a few yards away. The blonde was lying on her back and her mouth was fringed with the red froth from her torn lungs, for she had been shot through from side to side and the bullet couldn't have missed killing her instantly by much. Kane gazed down into her dimming stare, conscious of the awful fight that she was putting up to stay alive. He figured that she would find it easier to breathe if he turned her onto her right side — and he made to do just that — but she managed to gasp out that he shouldn't touch her and then added: 'All or nothing, Adam. I told you.'

'That you did,' Kane agreed glumly, 'and you've surely got yourself lots and lots of nothing. Why didn't you stop when I called to you back there? If you had, you wouldn't be in the state you're in now. Yes, yes — I know; all or nothing. Hell, I'd have still done all in my power for you — you know very well I would!'

'Adam, is an empty life worth living?' she queried, her bubbling words only just audible. 'Empty — that's what my years have been. Empty — that's all they'd have ever been. I — I seemed to have a chance. One chance. That's what — what Jack Starbuck offered me. I had to seize it. Empty it was, and now it's ending so.'

'Empty is what life is!' Kane railed at her. 'It's the space we live in. It's what we fill that hole with that counts. It's all up to us, Jilly. All of it!'

'If you say so,' the girl murmured, clearly not believing a word he'd said — and almost at the end.

Then he saw a change in her face, and realized that she was looking beyond him to something that was happening at his back. He knew that she was deeply afraid for him, and seemed to hear her mind shrieking at his own.

He spun round at his fastest, instinctively going to the draw, and his Colt was already cocked and rising as he saw that Alonzo Barris was now sitting up and had just drawn a sneak pistol from the top of his right riding boot. The colonel began lifting the derringer, but he got no further than that, for the sheriff's revolver boomed and the bullet from it pierced the Yankee's skull from front to back, scattering blood and brains all over the grass behind him. Then slowly — and even resignedly — his torso fell backwards and came to rest on the earth, leaving him flat and ready for his coffin.

Kane walked up to the corpse, his pistol hanging down the side of his right leg and smoking. It was then that he saw the bullet-hole in the front of Barris's coat and almost directly over his heart. So the varmint should have been dead since the middle of last night. That bullet of Jack Starbuck's had clearly flown straight and true. Why, then, hadn't the son-of-a-bitch died like any other son-of-a-bitch? Kneeling, Kane opened the front of the colonel's coat and saw the reason at once, for sticking out of the man's inside pocket was a steel cigar case which had stopped the slug inches short of a heart that was as black as they came. Evil as he was,

Barris had been given a second chance, but he hadn't had the sense to take it. Maybe it had been all or nothing with him too.

The sheriff retraced his steps to where Jill Pedlar lay. She was gone also. He stared down at his revolver, then put it away; and after that he gazed at his empty hand, seeming to see the whole of himself in the veined flesh. He wondered about the blonde and how she had saved him. 'Redemption, Jilly?' he asked. Who could tell? 'Thanks anyhow.'

It was time he went home. The bodies could be picked up later. The dead were beyond further harm. His deputy could drive a waggon over here and make the collection. Maybe the brush with reality would take the smart-ass smile off Jim Derby's face. Kane chuckled sourly at the thought. He was a cough drop and no mistake; but few men who took up sheriffing had very sweet or charitable natures. Besides, he could still smell that canvas bag which held the treasure of the Lone Star. Perhaps that stench was a message to the whole damned world of men — and a warning.

## THE END

## Other titles in the Linford Western Library

### THE CROOKED SHERIFF
### John Dyson

Black Pete Bowen quit Texas with a burning hatred of men who try to take the law into their own hands. But he discovers that things aren't much different in the silver mountains of Arizona.

### THEY'LL HANG BILLY FOR SURE:
### Larry & Stretch
### Marshall Grover

Billy Reese, the West's most notorious desperado, was to stand trial. From all compass points came the curious and the greedy, the riff-raff of the frontier. Suddenly, a crazed killer was on the loose — but the Texas Trouble-Shooters were there, girding their loins for action.

# RIDERS OF RIFLE RANGE
## Wade Hamilton

Veterinarian Jeff Jones did not like open warfare — but it was there on Scrub Pine grass. When he diagnosed a sick bull on the Endicott ranch as having the contagious blackleg disease, he got involved in the warfare — whether he liked it or not!

# BEAR PAW
## Nevada Carter

Austin Dailey traded two cows to a pair of Indians for a bay horse, which subsequently disappeared. Tracks led to a secret hideout of fugitive Indians — and cattle thieves. Indians and stockmen co-operated against the rustlers. But it was Pale Woman who acted as interpreter between her people and the rangemen.

## THE WEST WITCH
### Lance Howard

Detective Quinton Hilcrest journeys west, seeking the Black Hood Bandits' lost fortune. Within hours of arriving in Hags Bend, he is fighting for his life, ensnared with a beautiful outcast the town claims is a witch! Can he save the young woman from the angry mob?

## GUNS OF THE PONY EXPRESS
### T. M. Dolan

Rich Zennor joined the Pony Express venture at the start, as second-in-command to tough Denning Hartman. But Zennor had the problems of Hartman believing that they had crossed trails in the past, and the fact that he was strongly attached to Hartman's Indian girl, Conchita.

# BLACK JO OF THE PECOS
## Jeff Blaine

Nobody knew where Black Josephine Callard came from or whither she returned. Deputy U.S. Marshal Frank Haggard would have to exercise all his cunning and ability to stay alive before he could defeat her highly successful gang and solve the mystery.


# RIDE FOR YOUR LIFE
## Johnny Mack Bride

They rode west, hoping for a new start. Then they met another broken-down casualty of war, and he had a plan that might deliver them from despair. But the only men who would attempt it would be the truly brave — or the desperate. They were both.

## THE NIGHTHAWK
### Charles Burnham

While John Baxter sat looking at the ruin that arsonists had made of his log house, a stranger rode into the yard. Baxter and Walt Showalter partnered up and re-built the house. But when it was dynamited, they struck back — and all hell broke loose.

## MAVERICK PREACHER
### M. Duggan

Clay Purnell was hopeful that his posting to Capra would be peaceable enough. However, on his very first day in town he rode into trouble. Although loath to use his .45, Clay found he had little choice — and his likeness to a notorious bank robber didn't help either!

## SIXGUN SHOWDOWN
### Art Flynn
After years as a lawman elsewhere, Dan Herrick returned to his old Arizona stamping ground to find that nesters were being driven from their homesteads by ruthless ranchers. Before putting away his gun once and for all, Dan forced a bloody and decisive showdown.

## RIDE LIKE THE DEVIL!
### Sam Gort
Ben Trunch arrived back on the Big T only to find that land-grabbing was in progress. He confronted Luke Fletcher, saloon-keeper and town boss, with what was happening, and was immediately forced to ride for his life. But he got the chance to put it all right in the end.

## SLOW WOLF AND DAN FOX:
### Larry & Stretch
### Marshall Grover

The deck was stacked against an innocent man. Larry Valentine played detective, and his investigation propelled the Texas Trouble-Shooters into a gun-blazing fight to the finish.

## BRANAGAN'S LAW
### Alan Irwin

To Angus Flint, the valley was his domain and he didn't want any new settlers. But Texas Ranger Jim Branagan had other ideas. Could he put an end to Flint's tyranny for good?

## THE DEVIL RODE A PINTO
### Bret Rey

When a settler is cut to ribbons in a frenzied attack, Texas Ranger Sam Buck learns that the killer is Rufus Berry, known as The Devil. Sam stiffens his resolve to kill or capture Berry and break up his gang.

## THE DEATH MAN
### Lee F. Gregson
The hardest of men went in fear of Ford, the bounty hunter, who had earned the name 'The Death Man'. Yet even Ford was not infallible — when he killed the wrong man, he found that he was being sought himself by the feared Frank Ambler.

## LEAD LANGUAGE
### Gene Tuttle
After Blaze Colton and Ricky Rawlings have delivered a train load of cows from Arizona to San Francisco, they become involved in a load of trouble and find themselves on the run!

## A DOLLAR FROM THE STAGE
### Bill Morrison
Young saddle-tramp Len Finch stumbled into a web of murder, lawlessness, intrigue and evil ambition. In the end, he put his life on the line for the folks that he cared about.

## BRAND 2: HARDCASE
### Neil Hunter

When Ben Wyatt and his gang hold up the bank in Adobe, Wyatt is captured. Judge Rice asks Jason Brand, an ex-U.S. Marshal, to take up the silver star. Wyatt is in the cells, his men close by, and Brand is the only man to get Adobe out of real trouble . . .


## THE GUNMAN AND THE ACTRESS
### Chap O'Keefe

To be paid a heap of money just for protecting a fancy French actress and her troupe of players didn't seem that difficult — but Joshua Dillard hadn't banked on the charms of the actress, and the fact that someone didn't want him even to reach the town . . .

# HE RODE WITH QUANTRILL
## Terry Murphy

Following the break-up of Quantrill's Raiders, both Jesse James and Mel Becher head their own gang. A decade later, their paths cross again when, unknowingly, they plan to rob the same bank — leading to a violent confrontation between Becher and James.


# THE CLOVERLEAF CATTLE COMPANY
## Lauran Paine

Bessie Thomas believed in miracles, and her husband, Jawn Henry, did not. But after finding a murdered settler and his woman, and running down the renegades responsible, Jawn Henry would have time to reflect. He and Bessie had never had children. Miracles evidently did happen.

## COOGAN'S QUEST
### J. P. Weston

Coogan came down from Wyoming on the trail of a man he had vowed to kill — Red Sheene, known as The Butcher. It was the kidnap of Marian De Quincey that gave Coogan his chance — but he was to need help from an unexpected quarter to avoid losing his own life.

## DEATH COMES TO ROCK SPRINGS
### Steven Gray

Jarrod Kilkline is in trouble with the army, the law, and a bounty hunter. Fleeing from capture, he rescues Brian Tyler, who has been left for dead by the three Jackson brothers. But when the Jacksons reappear on the scene, will Jarrod side with them or with the law in the final showdown?

# GHOST TOWN
## J. D. Kincaid

A snowstorm drove a motley collection of individuals to seek shelter in the ghost town of Silver Seam. When violence erupted, Kentuckian gunfighter Jack Stone needed all his deadly skills to secure his and an Indian girl's survival.

# INCIDENT AT
# LAUGHING WATER CREEK
## Harry Jay Thorn

All Kate Decker wants is to run her cattle along Laughing Water Creek. But Leland MacShane and Dave Winters want the whole valley to themselves, and they've hired an army of gunhawks to back their play. Then Frank Corcoran rides right into the middle of it . . .

# THE BLUE-BELLY SERGEANT
## Elliot Conway

After his discharge from the Union army, veteran Sergeant Harvey Kane hoped to settle down to a peaceful life. But when he took sides with a Texas cattle outfit in their fight against redlegs and reb-haters, he found that his killing days were far from over.

# BLACK CANYON
## Frank Scarman

All those who had robbed the train between Warbeck and Gaspard were now dead, including Jack Chandler, believed to be the only one who had known where the money was hidden. But someone else did know, and now, years later, waited for the chance to lift it . . .